Infidelity

Also edited by Marsha Rowe

Spare Rib Reader
Sex and the City
So Very English
Sacred Space

Infidelity

Edited and introduced by

MARSHA ROWE

Chatto & Windus
LONDON

Published in 1993 by
Chatto & Windus Ltd
20 Vauxhall Bridge Road
London SW1V 2SA

A CIP catalogue record for this book is available from
the British Library

ISBN 0 7011 4463 1

Beyond the Blue Mountains by Penelope Lively was commissioned
jointly by *Traveller* magazine and the BBC.
It was published in *Traveller* magazine and broadcast on Radio 4.

Filmset in Linotronic Garamond Original by SX Composing Ltd,
Rayleigh, Essex
Printed and bound in Great Britain by Mackays of Chatham PLC,
Chatham, Kent

CONTENTS

INTRODUCTION

These ten stories of infidelity are set in bedrooms, town, cities, the world over. They range from a Perverse Writers' Conference in Boston to strange places such as Gary Indiana's 'Land's End' which seethes with fantasy like a witch's cauldron. There's Krakow in the late 1960s, in a satirical story of nationalist ferment and sexual freedom, and nineteenth-century colonial Hobart, where a true tale gives an unexpected twist to jilted romance. And there's Frankfurt, Florence, London, Buenos Aires.

Infidelity need not be of the sexual kind. It has many faces. Some of the stories echo the distant past in which feudal loyalty to a master or a creed embraced the dialectic of the oath and its renunciation. These stories extend the idea of infidelity into the political and cultural arena. In Nina Fitzpatrick's story, 'Mounting the Barbarian', the opponent – or 'infidel' – is Russian. He is the cultural other, the 'barbarian'. In David Widgery's story, 'Mea Culpa', the infidelity is political. There are stories in which sexual infidelity appears in the foreground, and others where the emphasis is on different aspects of a personal relationship. In Scott Bradfield's 'The Space Generator' the infidelity is between two sides of an individual personality. The conflict between liberty and loyalty is fought out as much within the mind of the protagonist as it is projected on to others. The 'infidel' may be both the enemy without and within.

The old double standard whereby, in marriage, husbands' infidelity was forgiven whilst wives' was forbidden, dies hard. Back in the eighteenth century Samuel Johnson said, 'Wise married women don't trouble themselves about infidelity in their husbands.' These days it seems that wise voters don't trouble themselves about the sexual infidelities of their parliamentary representatives. Certainly, we are moving closer to the attitude held by the French, that adultery is a private affair, of no concern to anyone but the couple involved. But adultery is still grounds for divorce, and in the minds of most people the ideal of a monogamous relationship is more popular than ever. Yet, in daily life, it appears that serial monogamy (more than one monogamous relationship, as in divorce and remarriage) is replacing the lifetime marriage. And it appears that many people prefer cohabitation rather than risk marriage, so tattered are its credentials.

In Alison Fell's story, 'The Grip', the heroine turns our attention back to the demand for fidelity. In a passionate soliloquy Anya, a young opera *assistante*, scorns her lover's insistence on his right to sexual freedom. She desires a monogamous relationship and protests that her lover wants a woman to be his equal but on terms that are exclusively his. While he may be a Don Juan, she refuses to be like those other stars/mistresses, victimised in libretto after libretto: 'Violette, Mimi, Gilda, Tosca, Norma, Isolde, Brünhilde. The catalogue of deaths. Nine by knife, three by fire, two who jump, two consumptives, three poisoned . . . '

Infidelity may be the only way to break in the new, the freshly possible as when, back in the 1960s, women claimed for themselves the right to pursue sexual desire without guilt, as men had done for centuries.

Infidelity need not be secret to fuel desire. In Jane DeLynn's 'Faithfully Yours', the hero is a gay woman who desires infidelity. She is adopting the code that infidelity in a relationship is neither exceptional nor dishonest. On the contrary, infidelity is self-recognition. It is not lying to oneself. Thus she is proud of her display of irony, of her self-detachment and lack of sentimentality. Heroes, female or male, need fidelity to the self to explore the trail of infidelity to another.

In so doing, perhaps, they discover fidelity is the goal. Yet, as we follow this female hero's dissection of her sexual identity through its ambiguities, shifts and transitions, we start to wonder whether her questions conceal as much as they reveal. Where does identity reside? Is sexual identity synonymous with self? Does the modern quest for identity involve self-deception, for all its apparent sincerity?

This theme of self-betrayal is laid bare in 'The Space Generator' by Scott Bradfield. The infidelity here is to the self. The wife, Audrey, denies her real feelings for her husband. She cannot acknowledge her feelings so she cannot contain them. Her hostility leaks out into the surrounding space. Her psychological repression is like the alienation of alexithymia, in which the sufferer does not recognise, and is unable to name, his or her own quite ordinary feelings. Audrey experiences such a lack of self-belief that her identity implodes. Instead of a person there's an automaton. The so-called rational, thinking aspect of her psyche has won out over the emotional side. One facet of her character betrays the other. Therefore Audrey cannot be the mistress of her fate and is subjugated to her husband. As a couple she and her husband collude, play out a form of symbiotic infidelity in order to stay together. This is fragile ground. They walk on it fearful that the space will hold, keeping the truth at bay to maintain the illusion of authenticity.

Although men are likely to compartmentalise sex as if it were something quite separate from the rest of life and not part of a relationship, women are more inclined to keep infidelity a secret. It's as if by not admitting it to their partners they too can compartmentalise a sexual affair. But an affair relationship and a marriage relationship are intimately and inextricably linked, something beautifully demonstrated in Penelope Lively's 'Beyond the Blue Mountains'. In the transforming landscape of 'down under' – the analogy for her own unconscious – the wife suddenly realises the erotic potential that she previously thought belonged to her husband's mistress, with all the silken glamour she associates with that word itself, the 'mistress'.

Penelope Fitzgerald's story, 'The Means of Escape', is a classic story of infidelity, with a difference. The heroine is the mistress of a household. She has a housekeeper whom she has rescued from a life of penal servitude. It would seem that the housekeeper boldly sacrifices herself to save the mistress's honour. But she also cheats her mistress out of her own act of escape from a dull future of feminine servitude. No one is handed freedom on a platter. This infidelity is many faceted, each element highly polished by its own ironic retribution.

Irony darts in and out of many of the stories. It features in David Widgery's 'Mea Culpa', a story of infidelity to principles. The irony of the doctor, the central character, is at first a form of self-protection. As he starts to lose his faith in the politics that sustain him in his East End London practice, his ironic stance is eroded from within. At first he continues to believe in the people who are his patients and in the basic goodness of humanity. Eventually this belief, originally linked to his faith in the great communist countries, is proved by events to have been misplaced. The inner core of hope and humanism that lay behind his irony has gone. He is left with empty cynicism. He comes to recognise this with an awful understanding of his own infidelity – that he has lost faith with his own conscience. He finds the strength of will to tell himself that he still believes in the lives of the people, in his patients in particular. The political belief that has sustained him in the past will sustain him again. Then, with a terrible, ironical twist of fate, he dies before he can put this belief back into practice. By his own infidelity, the character of the doctor was, in the end, betrayed.

The 'Land's End' of Gary Indiana's story is, as its name suggests, a place on the edge of consciousness. It is an enormously murky and claustrophobic townscape where people are locked into cellars, or lurk in dark cemeteries and damp boarding houses. It's anarchic, always on the verge of going over the top, and features a writer hero, Dennis, whose Land's End is a pastiche of Bram Stoker's *Dracula*. Dennis has his facts madly wrong. The text of history escapes him. In this place of exaggeration and illusion, we are all lost children, prey to instinct and wild winds. The infidelity here lies in the submission to unbridled eroticism. The thrilling intensity of promiscuous sex is personified in the figure of the vampire (eventually unmasked as a character named Marcus), the dark hero of all Oedipal longing. It is sex half in love with death. It is vampirism that feeds until satiated, consuming the bodies of its victims. Thus eroticism betrays the body of desire. 'There are so many ways to dissemble a love affair,' Dennis sighs, as he half recognises that his dream of fidelity to Seth, whom he wishes to seduce, will always be that, a dream, that he's unwilling to move into reality, to give up his fantasy life in which there is always another boy down the hall.

In the centre of 'Land's End', like a spider in her web, sits an ogre-like character, the Widow Humphreys, the mistress of the boarding house. She is just one of the many versions of a Mother figure appearing in these stories. She is glimpsed in 'The Grip' by Alison Fell. And in 'Mounting the Barbarian' by Nina Fitzpatrick, she is the great-grandmother, whose perverse authority is outmatched wit for wit by the youthful heroine.

Through her voice, the character of the great-grandmother in 'Mounting the Barbarian', we hear Polish nationalism in all its ambivalence. On the one hand, contemptuous, prejudiced and atavistic and, on the other, courageous, ironic, resistant to Russian imperialism. The heroine's betrayal of her great-grandmother's morality by losing her virginity to a Russian, is a metaphor for her betrayal of the Mother Country. The sexual freedom claimed by the young woman is also a political freedom. She is 'unfaithful' to her country but faithful to her sex and youthful autonomy.

In 'Entiendes', Colm Tóibín moves the character of the Mother to centre stage. To her, the son decides to tell the true story of his sexuality. By claiming fidelity for himself, for the character of his body, his desire, he is demanding that she also recognise something about herself: the fact that she, the mother, has a son whose sexuality is not as she has assumed it to be. They sit in a hallway of reflections and shadows, of windows and polished glass. It shows us that this will actually be a scene of stillbirth – the mother remains trapped within her own narcissism. She cannot see what the son is telling her, but instead steals his words, his story. Yet, as in all the best fictions, there is no single interpretation. Is she also telling him something about his father? This mother is unfathomable. She keeps secrets and denies recognition of the other, just as when she writes, she writes novels without characters, without dialogue. Her world maps places, not people.

I was intrigued by the idea of infidelity to the maternal idea. In my story, 'The Expulsion', Tanya seeks to escape from her own role as mother. She visits Florence to see her lover, leaving her baby behind her. In front of images of Renaissance art, she is tormented, fearful of both bliss and abandonment, recognising she has merely replaced one baby with another. This jolts her out of her own bad faith.

Flickering behind these infidelity stories are the mythic figures, Penelope and Ariadne, the archetypal representatives of fidelity and infidelity. Penelope, the image of virtue, constancy and loyalty, who shunned her suitors by weaving her tapestry every day then unravelling it each night while she waited for the return of her husband, Odysseus. And Ariadne, the symbol of the betrayed lover, abducted and abandoned by Theseus, to whom she gave the thread and the sword, the means to find and kill the Minotaur and seek his way back out of the dark cavern.

These are archaic creatures, epic remnants, not to be found literally in the stories. They are not characters in any of the plots. Yet they are there like phantoms, prefiguring our sense of what constitutes faithfulness and unfaithfulness. The ancient apparition of infidelity was feminine – fickle, helpless, tyrannical. Today perhaps all we glimpse is her shadow falling away from us, since in these stories infidelity embraces a far wider spectrum than that of the moral ambivalence of the female.

Yet perhaps Penelope and Ariadne have drifted in unnoticed. Reading the anthology's stories I asked myself why the character of the Mother appears so often.

Perhaps she is present because, as the existentialists argued, the Other for us all is the female and, as has been pointed out by writers like Julia Kristeva, not just the female but the maternal. For it is the mother symbol that embodies the conflict between nature and culture, between the instinctual drives and the ego. And by implication, the conflict between the desires of the body (infidelity) and the constraints of responsibility (fidelity). These may be obvious, even simplistic antinomies, yet also fruitful ones.

Infidelity, these stories suggest, edges us a little out of our shells, towards a clearer understanding of the other, allowing us to transform the bonds of fidelity into those of trust and freedom.

MARSHA ROWE

ᔥ *Entiendes*

COLM TÓIBÍN

During her last years Mother grew obsessive about her work. She wrote nothing new, but took down all the old books and reworked them as though there was a chance that some publisher would bring them out in a new version. But she knew that there was no such chance as she sent a dusty old volume down to the stationery shop on the ground floor to be photocopied, and waited, and then set to work on each sentence until the photocopied pages came to look like trade routes or a map of the prevailing winds. She was lonely and sad and distant in those final years.

I am living here in her flat, sleeping in her bed, using, with particular relish, the cotton sheets that she was saving for some special occasion. But I have still never opened the curtains in her study, just as she never did. I turn on the dim chandelier or the old desk light if I am looking for something. I know the window, which must be very dirty now, looks on to Calle Lavalle, and if I open it I imagine there is a strong possibility that some residual part of my mother will fly out over Buenos Aires and I do not want that. I am not ready for it.

She has been dead now for some years; her bones are firmly locked away in the family vault. Recently, I have felt unwilling to join all the rest of them – the Garays, the Alsogarays, and the Randolphs – in that underworld beneath the ornate angel and the stone cross. I can imagine the vague stench of ancestors still lingering, despite everything, despite all the time they have been dead. Maybe I'll find my own place of rest.

She wanted me to be a professor. She liked the bookish part of me, the English tweed suits. She mistook my reserve and thought that it was real. She never understood that it was fear. She liked my teaching in the university, even if it was only two hours a week in what passed for a language laboratory. And when I lost those hours and worked solely in Academia San Martin, teaching repetitious English, she never mentioned it again, but saved it up to contemplate in her hours alone in her study, another aspect of the way things had declined. She was disappointed.

Maybe that is what lingers in the study, her disappointment and all the time she had alone to savour it and go over it in detail. Some of that dull energy is left there, and I can feel it when I go into the room and I still call it Mother.

A few years before she died I became interested in a man again. Jorge was one of my students at Academia San Martin and from the first day he paid special attention to me as I spoke. He knew that I was aware of him all of the time and that I liked him. He liked literature and read obsessively, and he knew who my parents were, although I do not think he had read any of their work except a sonnet by my father which is in an anthology.

I think that is why I was special for him, why he waited behind and came for coffee with me, why he lent me books and asked me about Spain and England and listened as though each word were important and would have to be remembered. And he was special for me because of the light brown of his eyes, the slow ease with which he smiled, the softness in him.

Mother noticed that I was happier, and asked me if I had a girlfriend. I told her that I did not. She laughed, as though the possibility caused her infinite mirth, and said I had, I had, she knew I had, and she would find out soon, even though she never went out, someone would tell her. I told her again that I did not.

I listened for a clue that Jorge might understand. That is the word they use here. *Entender.* To understand. There are other words too, but this is the one that is still most common.

Entiendes? you could ask and this would mean Do you? Are you? Will you?

Sometimes I became tense with worry that I might blurt it out, that I might summon up the courage to ask him. It would just take one moment to say it. 'There's something I want to ask you. I've noticed that you never mention girls like most men here do, and you never look behind at a woman who passes on the street, and there's something I've wanted to ask you, you may guess what it is . . . Do you understand? *Entiendes?*'

If he had said yes maybe I would not have wanted him. Who can tell? Maybe I wanted whatever part of him was unavailable. Maybe if he had understood I would have despised him. Maybe I am being too hard.

Three days of the week I worked long hours. I walked the streets as I have always done, and there were some encounters, satisfactory in their way. I felt pure pleasure at the prospect of going into a room with another man and holding him and being held, and no disappointment afterwards, just a nod, a brisk departure. See you sometime.

My mother stayed in bed until late and then gossiped with Leonora, who came to clean, then dressed and went into her study ready for the day's work. She bought a new portable typewriter – you could buy anything in those years the peso was so high – and set about rewriting the whole of *Tierra del Fuego*, all three volumes, which were first published just before the Second World War when she was in her twenties. For a few years it sold, and it was translated into German. There is a box full of German copies on the floor of her study.

I remember when I was told I could read it. I was twelve or thirteen. It was before my father went to Brazil. And they sat with me as I opened it. Your mother's first novel. You can read it slowly, try the first chapter and see how you get on. It will be easier than your father's poems.

She described this strange country in page after page. Now it seems monotonous and overdone and forced, but then I accepted that each sentence was an inevitable consequence of its predecessor. I read her story of the early ranchers, trying to recreate Europe in the middle of nowhere. Their loneliness for the old ways, their abiding gentility, their few possessions and their great wealth. She knew the land, she did not come to the city until she was a teenager. I still get dividends from the wealth of that land, but they are small and getting smaller. She, too, got dividends every quarter, but the real dividends for her came in memory and imagination. In her books the nine feet of topsoil, with not a rock or a pebble between the Andes and the South Atlantic, was the hero, the protagonist. Everyone else was merely mortal. Love affairs, battles with the Indians, everyday dramas were small compared to the sheer scale and flatness of the land. Her books for me when I went back to look at them were full of foolishness and sentimentality and wrong-headedness.

And this is how she came to judge herself in those last days in that dim study.

Before, the rewriting was technical, like doing a crossword, but now she was serious. She wanted to start the book again, she sat in her study until the small hours tapping at the typewriter keys. I could hear her as I tried to sleep.

Soon, she abandoned *Tierra del Fuego* and began to rewrite *El Silencio*, her last novel, which she finished before I was born. There's no need to describe things in detail any more, she said to me, do you know that? She kept close to her a book of Borges's stories and Ernesto Sabato's *El Tunel*, and she read sentences out loud to me over breakfast. It's much easier to write now, she said. I think I could learn, she said, but maybe I'm too old. You keep everything short, that's the rule.

I told Jorge about her and he tried to get some of her books at second-hand stalls, but he could not. Years ago, they told him, her books were everywhere, but now you never see them. I loaned him a copy of the first volume of *Tierra del Fuego*. Her vocabulary was extraordinary, he said, and her sense of colour and landscape. Sunsets were her speciality and the change of seasons. He knew why she was interested in editing the books. You could take out every other sentence, he laughed as he said this, at random throughout the book and it would be much improved. It would be better to leave out the people altogether. My mother, he said, had no talent for writing about people. The sky, clouds, the vastness of the plain were all hers, he said, but not the human heart.

What he said left me drained and despondent. I had not given him licence to be so harsh. Maybe I told him too many stories about how strange and difficult she was in those final years, sometimes I made him laugh about her antics, and he did not appreciate how close I was to her, how bound up I was with her fate.

It was the mid-1970s and the generals were in power, and nobody stayed out late, even though the cafés and bars still remained open, eerily waiting for the lone customer who had missed his train to finish up and go, or for time to pass, or for something to happen. But nothing happened. Or a great deal happened, but no one I know ever witnessed any of it. It was as though the disappearances we hear so much about now took place in a ghost city, a shadowy version of our own, and in the small hours when no sounds were made or traces left. I knew no one who disappeared, no one who was detained, no one who was threatened with detention. I knew no one who knew anyone who was a victim. And there are others like me who have written about this and come to the conclusion that the disappearances did not occur, or occurred on a lesser scale than we have been told. But this is not my conclusion.

My conclusion centres on the strange lack of contact we have with each other here. It is not simply my problem, but it is a crucial part of this distant place to which our ancestors came in search of vast tracts of land: we have never trusted each other, or mixed with each other. There is no society here, just a terrible loneliness which bears down on us all. Maybe it's possible that I could watch someone being dragged away in front of my eyes and not recognise it. I would somehow miss the point, and maybe that is what I did, and others like me did, during those years. We saw nothing, not because there was nothing, but because we had trained ourselves not to see.

I don't remember when precisely I began to go home straight after work, but I no longer went for coffee with Jorge at the end of class. In those years you moved carefully without knowing why, you watched out. It was something in the atmosphere, something unsaid and all-pervasive, rather than anything printed in the papers, or broadcast over the radio.

But I saw him often, none the less. He came to the house, and we went out for coffee at weekends. I watched for some sign from him. I expected him to mention a girlfriend. I watched him when girls passed for some sign of desire on his part, but there was nothing.

And so it went on.

His clothes were old-fashioned and formal, he dressed like someone from an earlier generation. I liked that about him. I imagined him in one of those old-fashioned bathing costumes that covered the torso as well, and I thought of the shape of him, and that was exciting.

A few times I found comfort in the city. I picked up a man and went home with him. It would always begin in the same way: a sharp glance at a stranger as he passed, a turn of the head, and then the watching and waiting as he stopped to look into a shop window and I walked nonchalantly towards him. And then the approach, the finding out if he had a place to go to, and then the setting out, conspirators laden down with desire. I remember one such encounter not for the sex we had, but because of a sound that came into the room as we made love, the sound of car engines revving over and over.

I asked my partner – my lover? – my co-conspirator? – what it was. He brought me to the window to show me the police station opposite and the cars outside, driverless but still revving, with wires going from the engines to the basement of the building. They need power, he said, but I still did not understand. They need extra power for the cattle prods, he said, and I still do not know if what he said was true, if that was one of the centres to which people were taken, and if we fondled each other and came to orgasm within moments of each other to the sound of the revving of cars which gave power to the instruments of torture. It made no difference then because I did not believe him, and in a way I remember the pleasure of standing at the window with him more than anything else.

It is only now years later that it seems significant, perhaps the only real sign I was ever given of what was happening all around me. I cannot remember the name of my companion that evening, the man I stood with at the window, running my hands down his back, but I have often wondered how he knew, or thought he knew, or he imagined, what the revving of the cars' engines meant in our city at that time.

My mother fell in the shower and broke her hip at the beginning of spring. It was the end of her, although she lived for two years more. When she came home from hospital she went back to her books and her typewriter, but she was weak and distant, as though she only half heard what I was saying, as though she heard too many other sounds to be bothered listening to me, unworldly ones, whispering intimations of her long eternity in the grave.

I needed to be with her so I dropped some hours at the Academia San Martin, and I stayed at home most of the time. Leonora came every day to do the cooking and cleaning. I helped Mother to dress, and wheeled her about the apartment as she pleased. Jorge often called to the house, he had begun to work in his father's business so he had a car and it was easy for him to come into the city and stay late. He told my mother about all the modern writers, loaned her books as he had once loaned me books, often some of the same books. Mother read them quickly so she would have something to say to Jorge when he came next time. It's the style, she would say, that's what I read for, the style. I don't care about the story.

One Saturday night, I accompanied him to the street. There were still some people taking a stroll, and we walked down Lavalle until there was no one around and then we turned and walked back up. I told him that I would like to go back to Spain, that I was happier there than I had ever been anywhere else. He was listening carefully, he was curious enough to agree to come for a beer. I talked more. I told him about the time I had been there, how free I had felt, not just because I was away from my country and my family. But there were other reasons. As he listened I could feel my heart thumping. I was going to do it. I was ready now.

There were other reasons, I said. People are more relaxed there about sex; everything is easier. In certain circles you can do what you like. If you wanted to go to bed with another man, to have an affair with him, no one would think any less of you. You could do that. In fact, I did do that, I said. I could hardly control my breathing as I spoke. I did go to bed with men while I was there, and in England too. Maybe I should go back there I said. He nodded, and looked away, and then took a sip of his beer. He said nothing. I waited.

And you, I said, have you ever been with a man? I almost ran out of the café as soon as I said it. I had sounded too casual, but now I did not know what to do. I was just desperate for him to say yes, or maybe, or I'd like to. Or just leave the silence, leave everything suspended. But he said no, and his tone was casual too, but sure of itself. No, he'd never wanted to go to bed with a man. He liked women. And did I like women too, he asked. I felt a terrible weight in my head, I wanted to find some dark corner and curl up. No, I said, no, I did not.

We had another beer. Your mother will be waiting, he said. Does she guess about you? he asked. Have you ever told her? I needed to tell him how much I had wanted him, how my hopes had depended on him and that now things would change and I did not know how. But he was worried about my mother. I wanted him to go and leave me there, and I should have asked him to go. He talked as though nothing had happened. It was hard for my mother, he said, but I wasn't listening properly and I didn't understand what he meant. People have been saying that all of my life: how hard it is for my mother, my father's disappearing like that, vanishing.

She's had a hard life, he said. I realised as he spoke that he could have been fifty years my senior, he was so responsible and serious. I got a flashing vision of our country and Jorge as the main force operating, cut off from the real world, but mimicking its customs and habits. He looked like a parody of something as he sat there and tried to discuss my mother with me. And maybe I looked like a parody of something too: a homosexual in early manhood whose father ran away to Brazil and left him with his greedy, capricious mother. I was going to tell him that nothing my parents did to me or to each other had made me as I am. I have always been like this. When I was a baby I was homosexual. And I laughed to myself at this vision of myself in a pram.

He asked me what I was laughing at and I said that everybody always felt sorry for my mother, but they were usually older people – the maid Leonora, or friends my mother used to have – but I never expected him to join the chorus, and I found it funny that he had done so. I should tell her, he said, about myself. It was important for both of us. Before she died, he said. I would always regret it if I didn't. It would make everything easier.

And she would understand, he said. I laughed and stood up and told him that he could tell her himself, and since he liked her so much maybe he could change places with me and become her son and help her to put her clothes on in the morning and take them off at night. I, in turn, could take over his father's business and live in the suburbs.

He continued to call round. I was still interested in writing then and ordered new novels in English from the United States. He tried to read the books in English, but he could not. His grasp of the language was not strong enough. He suggested I translate a few short stories, but I found that the two languages were not compatible, I needed to change too much to make it work, and I began to rewrite the English sentences just as my mother was doing to her own prose of thirty years earlier. But after a few pages I grew bored.

I told Jorge how easy it was to pick a man up in the street. I asked him to check out the toilets in the railway station for himself some day if he didn't believe me and see if he noticed anything. He became worried about me. What if I were caught? If I went home with the wrong type? If it were a policeman just checking me out? It would kill her, he said. It would kill your mother. What would it do to me? I asked him, but he shook his head and told me that I must be careful.

Her hip did not mend and it began to pain her a good deal especially at night and it was hard for her to sleep. But she was alert all of the time, and even did some more rewriting on *El Silencio*, but none of it worked and she must have known that and become resigned to it. She was mellow and quiet for much of the time, sitting in the hallway in her wheelchair looking out at the sky and the back of buildings and the cats that manoeuvred their way along the ledges and rooftops. She read, until her eyes grew tired and then she needed me to talk to her.

The hallway looked like a porch with its huge window which

gave light to the living room during the day through a glass partition. Mother enjoyed being sandwiched between these two pieces of glass and we turned on a lamp in the evening until everything seemed all shadow and reflection. One evening as we sat there – it was nearly time for her to go to bed – she asked me about Jorge, she said that she liked him and wondered if I enjoyed his visits. I said that I did. Did I know much about him? she asked. Had I been in his house, for example, or met his family? I grew uncomfortable as she spoke, I did not know where the conversation was leading, and I did not want her to criticise him.

Had it ever occurred to me, she asked, that he was homosexual, and that was why he came? She looked at me sharply. I looked straight into the glass of the window and saw her shape in the wheelchair. No, I said to the glass, no it had not occurred to me. Well, I think he is, she said, and I think that it's something you should consider.

I stood up and walked through to the bathroom and closed the door behind me as though something was following me. I wet my hands and my face and stared into the mirror. I stood up straight. I was breathing heavily. I looked at my own eyes and then turned and opened the door. I did not stop walking as I began to speak; she turned and watched me, her expression defiant, unafraid, and that made things easier.

Jorge is not homosexual, I said to her. I am the one who is homosexual and I always have been. She did not flinch as I spoke, but held my gaze. I stood still. I invited him here, I said, because I believed, like you, that he was homosexual. But we were both wrong. Weren't we?

By this time I was standing in front of her shaking, and I felt like kneeling and burying my face in her lap but I could not do that.

She smiled and then shook her head in wry amusement. Somewhere in her face there was utter contempt. She sighed and closed her eyes and laughed again.

It has been so difficult for me, she said, and now this, now this, now this.

Now this, she repeated, and stared at herself stoically in the polished glass of the window. I stood there in silence.

So tell me about it, she said. Sit down here, she patted the chair beside her, and tell me all about it. Maybe we should stay up late tonight, she said. We still have time.

I looked at her in the glass as I spoke, and I told her what I could, and sometimes she asked a question. What I said became distant from us, as though I was reading from a book, or reciting a story I had been told. We were actors in that beautiful old tiled hallway night after night as we settled down to lurid tales of a wayward son at home and on his travels. His mother listening, infinitely patient, but not reacting, as though she would hear it all out before retiring to pass judgment.

I told her about London and being penetrated for the first time in a stranger's bedsitter, the shock of the pain and then the discomfort giving way to slow pleasure. She seemed more interested in Barcelona, where I had gone afterwards taking the map she and my father had used on their honeymoon, with the hotel where they had stayed, and other places, bars and restaurants, clearly marked.

He was gone more than ten years then and we had no idea where he was, and I wondered if he could be here in these streets, or whether he was still in Brazil from where he sent me a postcard more than five years after he left. He was on my mind as I walked the streets. The landlady marvelled at how tall I was. I must be Basque, she said. Only Basques have freckles like you. I must have Basque blood, she said, when I told her that I was Argentinian. Garay is a Basque name, she said.

I went out for a walk one evening when it was dark. I stopped at a bar on the corner and had a glass of wine and an omelette. It was a warm evening and I was wearing just a shirt and a waistcoat, light trousers and sandals. I was strolling along thinking about nothing.

As I told her the story Mother closed her eyes and listened. Sometimes she asked questions, made me fill in details, for example whether all this had occurred during my first trip to Europe or the second. I answered her and continued.

I noticed these two men coming towards me. I think that I noticed them because the younger one was so good-looking and because they both stared at me. But I was used to people staring at me because of my freckled face and my blond hair and my height. They held my stare as we passed, and they turned as I turned and I knew what it was. For a moment I was afraid and thought of heading back, going home. I sat down on a seat and as they came towards me I felt a surge of pleasure at the intense heat of their concentration. I knew who they were.

Where are you going? one of them asked me as he approached. The other stood back and smiled. They were relaxed. I'm just going for a walk, I said. I'm just wandering around. And then it began, the exchange of details, where I was from, where I was staying, my name. They lived near by, they said, and I agreed to go with them, and we tried to walk to the Plaza Réal as though we had known each other for years, but anyone could have spotted, I think, that we were strangers who were excited by each other.

We drank a beer, I think, in a large room overlooking the square. It was mainly furnished by a large mattress on a base and some other smaller mattresses. When the other one left the room, the beautiful one began to kiss me. I could taste the garlic on his breath and the sweat on his body. My tongue played with his tongue and my hands strayed over his body. I stopped as soon as his friend came back, but they told me there was no problem. He would go out and leave us. He waved as though he was far away as he went out of the door.

Soon we had taken our clothes off and were on the bed. He wanted me to fuck him. He took some cream from a drawer. At first it was too much for him. I was going in too fast, he said, and hurting him. So I started again, kissing his neck and his ears until he turned his face around and I could reach his lips. I kissed him gently and then I entered him slowly. He winced and called out, but it was gentle. I did not push until later when he was more relaxed. I put my arms around him and held him.

After I came I could feel him tighter than before. I pulled out and turned him round and kissed him and we lay there listening to the sounds from the square.

I met them again two nights later, but this time the beautiful one left me with his friend. This, then, was the bargain they had made. He would not let me fuck him, but it was good being with him, it was better than with his friend, more playful and exciting.

They left a note with my landlady, asking me to call around the next evening. This time there were a lot of people there, all men, all young and desirable. After a while, we broke up into pairs as people began to strip. I was embarrassed, this wasn't what I had expected. Also, I was excited by everybody, I could not make a choice, and what I remember about the man I lay down with was his thighs, their smoothness and shape. Some of them made jokes about me, the whiteness of my skin, my freckles, my dick. But it was funny and affectionate.

This was a game, no one fucked, we just lay with each other, fondling each other's bodies, talking, laughing, becoming excited for a while and then relaxing. I grew bored with my partner and wanted to move, but no one else seemed to do this so I was unsure if I could. I excused myself and went to the toilet and came back slowly and gingerly, meeting a boy in the passageway. He was different from the man waiting for me on the mattress, his torso was white and bare, and he was stocky with large legs and buttocks. I looked at him and understood his gaze in return. We embraced and found a place to lie down together.

I told her stories late into the night, embellishing nothing, sticking to the facts. She closed her eyes and put her head back as though she was taking in the sun, and she stopped me throughout if she needed a detail filled in. What happened to the boy I had abandoned? for example. What did I do the rest of the time in the city, did I ever catch any diseases?

Each morning when I woke I felt guilty, as though the telling had made it all wrong, but by evening the guilt had gone as we sat after supper in the hall. Usually, she signalled if she was tired, and I stopped and helped her to get ready for bed.

She went back to her work after a while. I could hear the sound of her typing when I came in from the Academia San Martin. I believed that this rewriting would bring her only sorrow and frustration, but nothing I could say would change her mind, and she did not tell me what she was working on.

In those months before she died she said nothing to me about what I had told her. I did not know – indeed, I do not know – what she thought of me, whether she was shocked and disturbed, or relieved and amused by the stories I told her. I wanted to say something about it, but in her final weeks she lost the power of speech, or elected not to use it.

And I was shattered by her death. We still had unfinished business. I had unburdened myself to her and got nothing in return.

I left her study in darkness, arranged for Leonora to come twice a week instead of six days a week as before and hired a lawyer to find out if my father could be declared officially dead. I decided to have his name and dates etched on the family mausoleum under hers. I decided to give him the same date of death as my mother. There was no law, as far as I knew, preventing me from doing this, but even so I expected a postcard to come in the door some morning with news from him, as I have done all my adult life. A card in our box in the hallway. One card.

I went through her papers, but there was nothing I could throw out. Maybe students of prose in the future will be interested in how this obscure old woman tried to change her work in her old age, but I think not. Students of prose will have other, more interesting things to do. When I die, or leave here, the papers will be thrown away. Maybe I shall have the courage to throw some of the stuff out myself before I, too, grow old.

It is the springtime of the year here in the southern hemisphere. There is pale sunshine in the day. I sit in the hallway in her chair writing this on a pad.

My mother told me nothing, as I have said, about what she was doing in her study during her last months and I did not ask. But after she died I found out one evening while I was idling through the drawers in her desk.

I came across a pile of paper on which the type was darker and clearer than was usual. She must have changed the ribbon. Slowly I began to read and was surprised by the opening paragraphs because they were not in her usual style or her usual setting.

And I sat back, breathless, as I realised what she had done. She had written the story of her honeymoon in Barcelona. She had described the streets, the hotel where they had stayed, the restaurants they had frequented. She was always better on settings than people, as Jorge pointed out, and the atmosphere of the city is more alive, maybe, than the couple on honeymoon.

But I know who they are, so it does not matter. I can fill in the details.

As I turned the pages that night I saw that there was a twist to her story, and I knew why she had been listening with so much dry attention to what I was telling her about my life, things I believed that I would never tell anyone. I felt cold first and shivered as I read, and then everything became clear about her. Suddenly, I remembered everything and saw everything. She was in the room hovering as if she were in every cell of my body.

In her story the husband one day leaves his newly wedded wife in the hotel and walks in the city. It is late, according to her story . . .

As I read, I realised the scene she was now setting, the event she was recounting. As I read, I followed my own account of my life in the city and I found that she was telling it word for word as I had told it. I was startled by her memory, and her determination to find a new story to tell before she died.

She used every word I told her, every detail about that room in the Plaza Réal and those men. But it was my father who walked naked across the room and switched partners, not me.

In her story my father returned to the hotel after each episode pretending that nothing had happened, and then disappeared back to the underworld of the city at an appointed hour each day. It peters out then. She died before she could finish it.

I can see my own face in the glass. It is daylight now and ghosts do not walk during the day. I am comfortable here. I am glad that I am alone, and she is gone, locked away in her room. Some day soon I will open the curtains and let her fly out.

∾ *Mounting the Barbarian*

NINA FITZPATRICK

In the autumn of 1967 a cloud in the shape of human buttocks appeared over Krakow. Towards evening the cloud reddened and the angry rump drew more and more spectators into Mariacki Square. People pointed and laughed, but their jokes were tinged with unease. They were used to various signs in the heavens, such as the Virgin Mary, bulbous rosary beads, Marshal Pilsudski on a white horse and flaming crosses. This, however, was quite unnatural. On previous occasions the sky had been serious and preoccupied with the best interests of our country, both national and spiritual. All of a sudden it had turned facetious and shamelessly taunted the people with a pair of muscular haunches.

What could it mean? The weather forecaster at the end of the TV news could barely suppress a giggle when she mentioned the cloud. It was an uncommon, though not unprecedented, meteorological phenomenon – possibly caused by toxic emissions from Nowa Huta. Most certainly it would disappear overnight. Then, gleefully: it was heading towards the east!

The following morning the cloud was still there, more

luminous and compact than ever. It had a yellowish tinge and seemed about to discharge itself on the city. Krakovians on their way to work stayed rooted to the ground. Some automatically opened their umbrellas though there was no hint of rain, others clustered in little groups to discuss the latest aerial developments. This time the jokes were fewer and people felt a little apprehensive, a little embarrassed. For how could you conduct your normal affairs in a normal way with a splendid yellow bottom displayed two hundred metres above your head? How could a boy say I love you to his girl in the presence of that ridiculous reminder of what, fundamentally, his love was all about? How could a procession of pilgrims heading for Jasna Gora go on with their Paters and Aves without falling into distraction and losing count? Weren't the Party Secretaries just a bit too literal when they claimed that the dark clouds hanging over our country were generated by imperialist and reactionary centres in West Germany and the United States. And what ran through the heads of the housewives as they stood for hours in queues for toilet paper outside the *drogeries* that morning?

As the day went on and the bottom in the sky failed to disappear, people were invaded by a vague sense of having committed some mortal sin which God was now bluntly pointing out to them. They had thought of themselves as a Promethean tribe, the crucified nation of Europe, the Irish of the east, the last Mohicans. But no! There it was, all native depravity, all the sloth, filth and corruption finally exposed. Passers by turned their heads in the street as if afraid to discover the truth in one another's eyes.

In the evening when the buttocks, as if tensing and straining, turned brick red once more, a preacher with a wooden cross appeared in Florianska Street. Godless atheists! Communist infidels! This is what you get for turning your back on the Almighty! You've turned your back on Him and He's turning his back on you!

A policeman with the help of two friars from the Mariacki Cathedral briskly hauled him away. The idea that God was flashing his arse to show his displeasure with Krakow was too preposterous to be endorsed either by the secular or religious authorities of the city. Besides, what would the French tourists buying imitation holy icons in the arcades think?

When dusk fell and the infamous sight melted into the darkness everybody sighed with relief. But the talking and guessing went on far into the night. Would the buttocks return the next day? How long would they last? Was Krakow about to suffer the fate of Sodom and Gommorah? And why Krakow and not Paris or New York?

'Why Krakow and not Paris or New York?' I asked Oblivia.

'I don't know,' she giggled. 'It's the finest pair of buttocks I've seen in a long time. It reminds me of Antoni.'

We were leaning on the window sill watching the apparition fade into the night sky. Our room was on the tenth and most dangerous floor of the student hostel. Everybody knew that the tenth floor was radioactive and that it was held together by a collective belief that it would not collapse just yet. Were it to collapse it would crush six hundred and fifty girls sprawled on rickety divans beneath and finally ravage the thousands of knickers that hung out to dry on lines over the bathtubs.

On the day the cloud appeared knickers became a favourite topic of conversation in the hostel. The whole building was giggling and guffawing. The approaching end of the world fired us all with apocalyptic excitements that not even the concrete and asbestos could quench. Oblivia was more in demand than ever. She spent the day rushing down to the phone in Reception and finally landed herself with three simultaneous dates. I felt a sickened, resigned jealousy. If the end came tomorrow I would perish pure as a parsnip.

'How will you manage?'

'I don't know,' she said absentmindedly, 'but since it may be the last time . . .'

Oblivia belonged to a special breed of women who answered I don't know to most things. That's why nobody called her Olivia but Oblivia. Rather than striving to be adequate in her responses she would say I don't know with so many different inflections, flavours and textures that most men found her disturbingly profound. There was no trace of guilt, no sign of embarrassment in her admissions of ignorance. On the contrary, there was self-confidence, discrete allusion, reproach even. She I-don't-knowed herself into the third year of law studies without special difficulties. Her mysterious response made some of her examiners ashamed of their questions and others more aware of their manhood. By holding out an empty head and silence to them she forced men to fill the disquieting vacuum with their own ideas. They had to make an extra effort, to surpass themselves even, and were then grateful to her for their own brilliance. To some unfortunates she became an addiction, a necessary void that vexed them into bad poetry.

I, by contrast, knew everything, remembered everything, had the facts beaten into me and nobody wrote poetry in my praise.

It was through Oblivia that I came to understand the effect women have on world affairs. As it happened, she was to miss her appointment with History. Unwittingly, on the night of the buttocks, she passed it on to me.

'Look,' she said, pulling on her stockings. 'I have an idea. I take Mateusz, you take Mikhail Sergeyevich and we dump Jozek.'

'Wait a minute! What Mikhail? I'm not going anywhere.'

'Don't make unnecessary difficulties. If you don't go he'll be very disappointed.'

'But it's you who have the date, not me.'

'He's never seen me, I've never seen him, so there's no problem. You go there, you drink a cup of tea, you talk about I don't know Pushkin or something like that. Besides you speak Russian better than I do.'

'A Russian?'

'Oh, don't panic. He's here with a delegation of lawyers from Irkutsk or Mlynsk or – oh, I don't know. A friend gave him my number. Besides, you're not going to tell me that you'll sit here all by yourself while everybody else goes balanga.'

She whirled towards the door in a blizzard of scent.

'The Europa Hotel. Downstairs restaurant. At eight.'

'Wait. How will I know him?'

'Oh yes. He says he looks sad and wears a grey jacket.'

A Russian! I needed to analyse the situation. Let's take the cup of tea first. If a girl is invited to a man's place for tea she doesn't refuse. Why – is she afraid of something or what? If she refuses it can only mean that she has a sick imagination. I had often been for tea to men's places and nothing ever happened.

But what if something happens this time?

A Russian? My great-grandmother did what she could to the Russians under very unfavourable circumstances in the times of the Tzarat. On Fridays she would hire two half-starved Russian soldiers for a rouble each to play with her children. She would order the soldiers to stand in the middle of the drawing room and then loose her offspring on them.

'Crush the Moscovites! Beat the shit out of them! Kill the bastards,' she screamed, shaking her fists.

And the children kicked and bit and beat the poor Sashas and Sergieys, who bore it calmly because it meant that their bellies would be full for another week. As for Great-Grandmother, it was her small retribution for the hangings and the deportations and the broken backs in the Siberian mines. *My dear sons, I went to war, just as your grandda went before, and grandda's father and his grandfather, to fight the savage Russian foe.*

What if Mikhail son of Sergiey son of Vania had come for his revenge?

It couldn't be. We were now fraternal nations with clean blank pages in the history books instead of bestialities.

I was a virgin but I had no illusions. I was the kind of woman who had to be ravished. I was so full of myself that I could never yield to anybody without being forced. I had to be taken against my will. I knew that in my case rape of one kind or another was a historical necessity.

Looked at this way, Mikhail Sergeyevich was a godsend. He had dropped out of the sky especially to . . . No, no, that was going too far. But if he wanted to ravish me then his role as an imperial Russian would give him the bit of extra jizz. On the other hand, the fact that he was a barbarian would take the sting out of it. He was the elemental, the irresistible power of flood and fire. He was fate. He had come to Krakow, he would do the necessary, ravage the ravageable and go.

It would all be over in one night and then, sunshine or Apocalypse, I would at least die a woman.

And so, on the Night of the Cloud, I went to my deflowering in the Europa Hotel.

The hotel was illuminated for the occasion and there were elegiac flags of the Brotherly Nations hanging limply from the balconies. In the foyer I lost all my courage. Two women on a time fuse of peroxide, fishnet stockings and mini-skirts sizzled away in a corner and batted their thick eyelashes at me. One of them smiled. I cast my eyes down on the carpet. But there was no refuge there. A large oval drink stain leered up at me like an addled vulva.

I couldn't go ahead with it. Back in the safety of the hostel it had seemed an alluring prospect. But now I was mortified by the shamelessness of my own scheming. If I lifted my eyes I would see that everybody knew. Such a decent girl! And just imagine – with a Bolshevik. As if those vampires hadn't drawn enough blood from the nation already.

Apocalypse or no, I couldn't do it.

A group of pregnant men in non-iron shirts and nylon raincoats rotated towards the restaurant. They were like fat spinning tops wobbling at the end of a spin, bumping into one another cheerfully, lifting their bellies the way girls lift up their breasts. Their wives followed in kremplin dresses and loud smiles.

I slipped into the dining room in the eddy of the wives and found myself a corner table where I could keep an eye on everybody.

The restaurant was full of tipsy Krakovians and tourists on a final spree before Cosmic Closing Time. They sang obscene songs, broke the bread of wisdom and shared the chalice of remembrance. A sour lava of smoke, steam, and spittle billowed slowly from one corner of the room to the other. *We're a lava field, with surface cold and dirty, hard congealed, but there are fires beneath no years can end; let's spit on this foul crust and then descend.*

Our jaded national poems hung over me like a sentence.

I heard the familiar, sweet-brutal sounds of Russian coming from a table near the door. Two men were quarrelling. The third sat bathed in coppery light fingering his watch and, oh God, staring down into the secret recesses of his Slavic soul. *These people's bodies like thick fabric which nests the wintering caterpillar soul . . .*

Mikhail Sergeyevich, I was sure of it. He was broad faced, broad shouldered and very sad. A girl in an evening dress entered the dining room. Mikhail Sergeyevich's soul rose shimmering to his face – and sank back again as the girl called out raucously to her boyfriend at the bar. In that unguarded moment he emanated the infinite sorrow of the steppes and the birch groves and the viscoid flesh of boletus. I could smell it in the dining room air over the reek of cabbage and *pierogi*.

How could I go and introduce myself with Rosencrantz and Guildenstern leering in the background? They were drunk and they sniggered at Mikhail for wasting his best shirt on a Polish hussy. He bore their abuse nobly for a while, shaking his head and looking officiously at his watch. Finally, weary of their inanity and my absence, he got up and left the restaurant dragging his soul at his heels.

I made up my mind. I would allow Mikhail Sergeyevich to deprive me of my virtue. Russian or no Russian he was a man with a soul.

'Are you looking for someone Miss?'

The receptionist swept me with his one eye from head to toe.

'Yes. I mean no. I just wanted to leave a message, that's all. I'll come tomorrow.'

'Hee, hee, there might not be any tomorrow.'

'Oh, I'd forgotten.'

'Some cloud, what? As for myself I have survived three ends of the world. The First World War, the Soviet Revolution, the Second World War. Not bad going? And in the end this cloud will do for us!'

He leaned towards me, his breath stinking of Zubrowka.

'I'll tell you what it is. The Russians are testing a bomb. We're the guinea-pigs. That's what these bastards have come here for. They're here to test our reaction.'

'Why should they want to do anything like that?'

'Why? Because it's convenient. A little cloud will do the job for them. You need no army, no propaganda, no Jews, just a little cloud.'

A familiar chill runlet descended from my heart to my feet, a shiver of ice which foreboded many of my partial suicides.

'Excuse me. What is the number of Mikhail Sergeyevich's room?'

His face went pale but he stared at me with his unblinking brown eye.

'I have no such name.'

'Very well. What are room numbers of the Russian lawyers? I have an appointment.'

I could hardly stand on my two feet.

He hesitated for a moment and then gave me the numbers in a voice that excluded me from the land of the living.

I knocked twice on all the doors of the Russian corridor praying that nobody would answer. The radio was on and blasted soul-wringing songs through the walls. Like a dowser over a black spring I knew, my belly knew, when I stood outside Mikhail Sergeyevich's room.

I knocked again but he couldn't possibly hear me. My Guardian Angel was offering me every chance to retreat and flee the infamy. And yet I pounded on the door like a madwoman demanding defilement.

The songs came to an end but my resumed knocking was drowned by the 'News at Eight'. I opened the door and the imperialist war in Vietnam flooded out mixed with the scent of eucalyptus toothpaste.

Mikhail Sergeyevich in an open pink shirt stood to attention beside the handbasin and smiled at me with a mouth full of foam.

'The radio!' I shouted, pointing at the loudspeaker. He shook his head and helplessly spread his hands. I understood. We had the same radio in the student hostel: once on it couldn't be turned off by the residents.

I bowed a nervous, understanding bow. He bowed back to me, his smile widening. I bowed again, trying desperately to remember the Russian greeting which I had studied for thirteen years at school. And so we bowed back and forth like a pair of geese. We bowed and bowed until he burst out laughing. His gaiety carried me with him. Still giggling he pointed to the sofa with his toothbrush and returned to the handbasin to rinse out his mouth. He gargled and snorted and spat with great Russian fervour and satisfaction. He shivered and shuddered and threw cold water on his face.

I felt like a fillie waiting for the stallion. His roguish smile when he turned to me again confirmed that he looked on the matter in much the same way as myself.

He smiled gaily as if the centuries of monstrosity that lay between us had never existed. Generations of his ancestors had followed the plough and slept in haylofts. The murder of millions had given him the chance to keep his hands soft and to strut around hotel rooms in foreign countries.

There was no conflict in him – with the world, with himself –

no crack, no wound. Nothing blistered or bled in him as it should.

A hatred, not my own, stirred in my belly. Great-Grandmother shook her fist in my face and screamed, You slut! You Judas!

Very well. I'll have tea and I'll go.

We drank our tea philosophically, now and then nodding our heads as if to say: Isn't it a crazy old world we're living in? The radio gave out the high-water mark for all the major rivers in the country. Neither of us attempted to move beyond the pre-arranged idea we had of one another. We renounced without a qualm one another's geology. There were deep strata in both of us – Permian, Devonian, Silurian, Cambrian, Pre-Cambrian – which we tacitly agreed to leave unexplored. We stopped at the pencil-thin surface, the downs of the breast and haunches, the curve of the knee, the flair of the nostril.

I asked him for a cigarette but he misunderstood.

'Good,' he shouted against the radio, 'I see you don't like to waste time.' And he grabbed our glasses and emptied them out of the window on top of the banner of the German Democratic Republic.

He's going to do it now, I thought in a panic, and stood up.

'Sit down, sit down!' he cried, and I sat down obediently.

'Now let's see what we have here,' he winked at me and pulled out a bottle of Kalinka from his suitcase.

I was relieved. Perhaps I'll get plastered quickly and feel nothing. But what if I don't? My anxiety like a defenceless hairy moth blustered round the room and bumped into everything. It blustered for a little while, poor thing, and then it stopped.

'To the friendship of the Polish and Russian peoples!' he shouted and tossed back his vodka.

'Amen,' I said and followed suit. 'Amen.'

Mikhail Sergeyevich refilled our glasses and looked at me encouragingly.

'To the Polish Russian Combine-Harvester!' was the best I could manage.

He winked at me again and emptied his glass. I felt like crying. He was a stage Russian and I was a stage Pole and how could we possibly do it in this state?

'Do you want to see the town?' I shouted and stood up again in a last attempt to avert the inevitable.

'But it's night! You can't see anything at night!' he shouted looking at my bosom. 'To peace!'

'And the dove!'

'To the ladies of Krakow!'

'And the gentlemen of Siberia!'

His brows shot up.

'And their Five Year Plan!'

I saw the confusion in his eyes as he struggled to find the proper reaction. Will he throw me out?

He burst out laughing. He laughed and shook his head in bewildered approval. Once again his soul soared up and my soul leapt in recognition. For a moment we were suspended above the maw of History, the rage of the poets, the graves of the martyrs and my great-grandmother's unforgiving face.

All I could think of was my underwear.

I had put on the matching set with the sunflower pattern which I usually wore when going to the doctor. They were a diversionary tactic intended to confuse an invader with their cheerful innocence. Only a brute would lay hands on such trusting, open-eyed blossoms.

Mikhail Sergeyevich was a brute. Or perhaps he understood

that that was what was half required of him. He shouted a
militant *Na zdarowie*, emptied his glass and sat down beside me.
Now, I thought, and I saw the same word written in Cyrillic on
his broad Slavic face. Now.

I felt his hand moving up and down my back and then
unbuttoning my dress. He was blowing a mist of warm vodka
across my cold shoulder blades.

'Crush the Moscal!' screamed my great-grandmother. 'Pluck
out his eyes!'

I shrank into my sunflowers and they came off all the more
easily.

Of course I could scream but I didn't. Of course I could fight
but I didn't. I let him go on aware that the whole thing was both
necessary and ridiculous. The radio was broadcasting a repeat of
a programme called 'The Matysiak Family'. My mother and I
used to listen to the Matysiaks every Saturday evening. She was
listening to it now. She was sitting in her matronly chair beside
the radio, nodding her head and painting her fingernails. While
she nodded away Mikhail Sergeyevich butted me triumphantly
into a corner of the sofa. Just at the moment when Mrs Matysiak
was scolding her son for escaping from reality and my mother
was blowing on her nails he collapsed beside me, his face red as a
borstch soup.

No magic casements had opened on the foam of fairy lands
forlorn. No sun of liberation. Nor was my body temperature
higher. To tell the truth, Mikhail Sergeyevich hadn't noticed that
it was my first time and I had hardly noticed myself.

So, had I lost my virginity or not?

A disquieting thought, at first a little foul and hysterical, but
then more and more confident and triumphant, filled my mind. I
hadn't lost anything. If anybody lost anything it was the Russian.

After all, he had emptied himself with a howl into me and not me into him. He lay there unmanned and deseeded while I was ready to run to Planty Park and back. And how could anyone claim he had possessed me? What there was to possess, cuckoo spittle and snail slime, was inside me.

I put on my dress and left the room without a word. Mrs Matysiak was frying sausages for her husband. I felt a great tide of affection for her. I was back with my own people.

I ran through the miserly darkness of the People's Republic to Planty Park. I ran over the dead leaves in the acid frost of the October night. I thought about my bum and the celestial bum in the sky. I could sense it hovering reassuringly above me in the darkness. For a moment I was part of the great chain of being.

I tried to remember Mikhail Sergeyevich's face. However hard I tried I just couldn't call up his face.

Even today, however often I see that face on the TV screen, I can't be sure. For me Mikhail Sergeycvich, the man destined to destroy the Empire and to lead us all back to the nineteenth century, remains a headless horseman who rode me to nowhere.

❧ *The Grip*

ALISON FELL

ACT I
SCENE I

*In a Frankfurt apartment Anya, a young opera
assistante, reflects on her love affair with Tadeusz, a
renowned opera director. The action takes place in a
Spanish pensione, in the Nuremberg Opera House, and
on a mountainous ridge high above the Mediterranean.*

No, Tadeusz, I say on the telephone, don't come
tonight, and with those few flicks of the tongue I both
make absence and protect you from untold hungers
and angers.

More than anything, at my age, you said, a man
wants an equal in a woman. What you forgot to add,
Tadeusz, is that the terms of the equality are exclusively yours.

Così Fan Tutte, I say to myself. So he wants me to
toy with infidelity, so he wants me to steal the demon
of Don Giovanni, the sword, the importunate daring?

I too must be *Übermensch*,* your mirror, is this what's required? But will you be my mirror, Tadeusz? Will you be Donna Elvira for me, betrayed and abandoned yet still forgiving; powerless, swooning with despair, calling on just Heaven to protect her zealous heart?

More than anything, you said wistfully, a man wants an equal. But are you Elvira's equal, Tadeusz, in love and in passion, in *eros* and in *agape*? Oh she's a fool, yes, but a dignified one, in a world where men set themselves free for no other reason than to wave mad swords at their mothers!

Again and again, war breaks out. Don Giovanni as Byronic hero (your version), versus Don Ottavio – 'a puppet fiancé', 'a flimsy tenor', 'the biggest milksop in all opera'. Or else (my version) Don Giovanni as hysteric, Don Giovanni with his panicky phallus: rapist made revolutionary by generations of directors, of musicologists. (I have listened to too many explications of Mozart's sublime demon: tragedy offset by mischief.)

Again and again the chauvinist epithets fly: – You Germans with your self-righteous *angst*! – You corrupt and cynical Poles!

You take yourself too seriously, Anya, you say – meaning, simply, that I disagree with you, rub your nose in the red earth, remind you of blood, pain, abjection, embarrassing you. (For then where is your equal and how much is your liberty worth?)

* Superman

Ah che barbaro appetito,* Tadeusz! As a lover you should yield to the desires of the one who adores you, to this Anya who clambered up the boulders of the ridge that day – the ridge which bulged so alarmingly out over the sea – tearing hands and trousers on the harsh lacework of the limestone, breathless, beginning to tremble, keeping her back turned to the terrible drop.

(*Da qual tremore insolito sento assalir gli spiriti!*)†

Così fan tutte, Anya, you said. This is what we all do, no? Deceive.

In Nuremberg you leapt up on to the stage of the opera house, explaining, expostulating. Your hair bristled blue-black in the spotlights. *Despina, Despina, meine kätchen!* Miming first the walk of a gutsy serving maid, then the exaggerated prance of a tart. Discriminating. *Nach so soubrettish, ja?*

The Dutch singer stood with hands on her hips and feet pointed in high button boots, head tilted pertly at you. *Jawohl, Herr Direktor.*

The *prima donnas* were less amenable. Mozart can bore me, I have to admit, sulked Dorabella, and you threw your hands in the air, appalled. All the same, how skilfully you flirted, cajoled, sweetened the ample crinolined women. Fussed over the ugly yellow haystack that was Dorabella's wig, tweaked at a fichu,

---

* Such a barbarous appetite.
† What is this strange fear that now assails my soul!

listened gravely to a complaint about Fiordiligi's corse-
lette ... In the dark auditorium I took notes and
wanted to burst into tears for crushed love, for loneliness, for lack of a self which might be cosseted like
those definite women with their great thighs, their
great breasts which lent weight to their sulks and protests, their scarlet lips which quivered possessively, and
sullenly, and without restraint.

(In the opera the work of an *assistante* is poorly paid
and requires loyalty, discipline, forbearance. One must
keep the 'director's book', one must run the director's
errands, one must keep a grip on everything under the
sun while the director rushes here and there, to Munich
or Stuttgart or Vienna, to consult with costume de-
signers or audition singers for his next production. One
should also be pretty, hide one's ambitions, and never
complain.) No, I say, don't come, and immediately the
night is dark as a nest without a bird, the depths of it.
   On the ridge there were splashes of a bitter dark
grass which I could only grasp at the risk of lacerating
my hands, and, here and there in the crevices between
the sharp limestone boulders, the pale mauve heads of
winter crocuses. The sky was blue like summer and the
tongues of the ridge leaned out precipitously over the
sea. Yes, oh yes, I wanted to steal your demon there,
Tadeusz, under the incomparable sky, in the salt-
drenched air, I wanted to insert myself into your place.
Into your strong legs which moved on their sure trajec-
tory above me, into your bullish chest where the heart
thudded slow and even, into your scratched and

scarred fingers, into your hidden compartments of desire.

(In my family, Tadeusz, we weren't supposed to assert our own desires. Things had to *come* to us in the form of rewards for being good, unjealous, disciplined, unselfish, grateful. Never for being – *spoilt*, demanding, expressive. Desdemona's handkerchief lighter and whiter than a snowflake. Better to strangle her in the bed where she has sinned, cries Otello, while Desdemona, aghast, mourns the cloud which disturbs Otello's reason and her destiny.)

If I'm demanding, if I assert my direct desires, I cry, break down: first there's a rustling in my head, like mice in a wastepaper basket; then comes a silence as the tears, caught out, try to play dead, render themselves undetectable; finally – with a small aching fright which signals that I've abandoned this notion of myself as irreproachably meek and deserving – they flood down my face.

On the night before the ridge we had lain in each other's arms and listened to the clink of goat bells in the orange grove, and I said – bravely, I think – that I wasn't strong enough for this struggle, couldn't cope with your sworn principles, your stubborn free-loving, Tadeusz, do you hear me, your five other women, I can't make myself strong enough. In that case, you said, I'll have to make myself weaker. A promise which wrapped me like a nest all night long, until in the morning I remembered that my mother never wanted me to fling myself into her arms and in all probability would not have caught me.

(*Ah proteggete Voi la mia credulità.*)*

My mother, you see, was faithless, and the memory of this could still rob me of the vision which might have quieted my soul, up there on the ridge, a thousand feet above the snarling sea.

Earlier, looking up from the col, I had quailed at the sight of the pinnacle which leaned out over the waves.

(*Blood . . . it worries me . . . see them embrace . . . the handkerchief.*)

It will be easier than the traverse, you said. To go up. There were flecks of birds overhead, small pips of goat shit underfoot.

My mother, you see, was perfect, whiter and lighter than a snowflake. And if that day and in that same way you too seemed perfect up there, dancing across the pale curve of the boulders, it could only be because I had strangled that other whore, silenced her – at least temporarily – by gripping her round the throat.

That whore who is Otello's wife.

Squinting up at you, Tadeusz, I saw myself suffused, suddenly, by the dream I had had the night before: saw

* O God, protect my credulous heart.

an Anya dancing with happiness in a black dress with a
cleavage cut to the heart and an ample skirt embroi-
dered with wild spiralling roses, an Anya dancing for
the joy of having such a dress in which to exhibit herself to some unseen audience, jumping from chair to
bed to sofa – perfect balance – throwing her arms up in
abandon, perking out her breasts, thrusting her hand
through the wild hanks of her hair. Drunk, drunk with
happiness. And on the ridge a radiance sprang up from
my toes and spread through the sinews and muscles of
my legs to my belly, to my tingling breasts, for this fantasy Anya was ... what I had just achieved, with
wishes that, like hands which tie up Christmas parcels,
make up their own happy stories, was to create – out of
that chancely loving remark of yours, Tadeusz –
myself-as-winner, as she-who-is-loved, (things would
come to me), was to see myself as if through the ador-
ing, exclusive, passionate eyes of Tadeusz (you who in
reality have always sworn fidelity to a principle which
to me is cold and rationalistic, even manipulative, and
whose eyes *in reality* are eyes which wander freely
rather than eyes which settle on me and grow vivid
with feeling); what I had achieved was to create these
brimming eyes – although they were invisible, in
parenthesis, outside the frame somewhere – and fill
them with this vision of Anya in the rapturous dress.
And if in the real world the dress itself would be what
promised to establish this position as *prima donna*, as
first lady – (you must understand that in my family we
were never allowed to *compete*) – this place at the top
of the pyramid of many women – (glorious vertigo) –
and for this reason the dress would be bought and

hoarded and invested with magic and talked to as it gleamed from its hanger in the deep nest of the night – in the fantasy it was the eyes which came first, the eyes which, limpid with love, *allowed* the exhibition, the low-cut bodice, the wide smiling skirts, the black velvet grace.

It will be easier, you said, to climb over the pinnacle, and I thought: but where will my mother go, what part will be left for her, now that she has been relegated to the sidelines? (Where do people go, after all, when you excise them from your dream in order to insert yourself in their place?)

Oranges. Oranges fallen from the trees in the orchard and, between them, rows of bean flowers pie-bald against the green leaves, against the red earth. I wanted to be still at the centre, aligned in your arms like a stone at the heart of a date – a sweet containment which you in your restless ardour would have seen as a fate worse than death.

Below us, to the left – where I could bear to look – the valley was patched with stony fields and olives and the bleached ruins of irrigation ditches. On the right, I couldn't bear to acknowledge the sea or wonder what it would mean if you were to make yourself weaker *here* and *now*, with the buttress rearing above us like the stone belly of a horse, if you were to lose your grip and plummet with a trailing cry.

(*Dond'escono quei vortici di foco pien d'orror?*)*

* Whence come these hideous spurts of flame?

Listen to me, Tadeusz, I admit it. If I resisted you when you tried to make me a mirror-image of you, it was only because (secretly, wildly) I wanted to be, that day on the pinnacle above the sea. I wanted to conquer, to grip lightly, to balance as you did; I too wanted to certify my courage, my willingness to live. Similarly, when you fought that vision of need in me, those tears (fiercely), when you stood in the night bedroom waving your sword at me, what vortices of love and pity threatened to betray you?

(*Che contrasto d'affeti, in sen ti nasce!*)*

There was a wind, then, that rustled through the sharp grasses like mice, as if to signal the abandonment of some notion of myself, and my hair lifted, stood up on the vertical draught. The sky reeled above that Wagnerian crag, the wind groaned, I clung to the faithless rock. At such moments the soul lives in the stomach and is afraid of escaping.

How softly the oranges fell from the trees in the night, with a slight thud, into the red earth. Then, in the morning, there would be – around the bole of each neat tree – six or a dozen or more. The tree laying its eggs in the nest of the night . . . *abjection*, Tadeusz – a concept you run from in terror, even to the point of waving your sword at the stone belly of the horse. *Abjection*. The tree laying its bright eggs. Pity, duty, love. Donna Elvira's long cry swooping like a shadow across the night patio, *Ah chi mi dice mai quel barbaro*

* What a tumult of emotions afflicts my soul!

dov'e.* (She sounds like a book, Leporello mocks – like Mozart – constantly.)

Fidelity repels you, Tadeusz – fidelity suburban and sorrowful as brass umbrella stands. Your own mother was faithless, left you early and always, therefore you need nothing and will prove it over and over again. You will deny absence by becoming absence; space will gape behind you as you rush here and rush there, spitting three times for luck and the flight to freedom.

And yes, it was this freedom I sought when I stretched my arm up, groping for a handhold on the convex curve of the pinnacle, trying to grip it and cling on. But at my feet, then, two partridges erupted from the juniper scrub and flew loose dizzying horizontals out across the valley with its small dots of goats, its scattered marigolds too yellow for December, its lemon trees sheltered from the sea-bluster by the thousand-foot toothed crest of the ridge, its dead ploughs and its vanished houses. *Da qual tremore insolito*, Tadeusz. In the space of moments my courage had flared up, burnt out.

The song of my nerves carried me out, flailing, into thin air; my mother's voice, caressing, soared once more, and I was possessed, not knowing which heroine inhabited me or which tune of suffering haunted me. (Violetta, Mimi, Gilda, Tosca, Norma, Isolde, Brünhilde. The catalogue of deaths. Nine by knife, three by fire, two who jump, two consumptives, three poisoned, and on and on.)

Finire così, cries Tosca: To end like this! Weeping

---

* Oh, who can tell me now where is the treacherous knave?

over her dead Mario, over the execution which should
have been a fake but which turns out, traitorously, to
be real. And she flings herself, wailing, from the battle-
ments: the woman sings and the melody carries her
away.

My mother cups her empty hands on the card table
like a nest, making an absence which I must fill for her.
My mother, superseded, folds her hands. *Così fan
tutte*, no? This is what they all do, these *prima donnas*
past their prime. They flare up for men's eyes, burn
out, fade into silence and exile. Sit with the cards spread
out in a circular game of patience, while on the sideboard the letters from the daughter are displayed where
visitors will notice them, a thin faithless sheaf in a brass
holder with a swan's beak for a clasp.

In the space of moments I'm flayed by the rock, I
collapse, I weep, I'm afraid of irritating you, I can't get
a grip, I'm not in command of myself, my shoulders
feel broken. Is this bravery, Tadeusz, this sword waved
at the stone belly of the horse, the stone horse above
us?

You say that you love me, link me like music to my
mother's body, without mediation – but you love also
in Munich, in Stuttgart, in Vienna. *(Ma in Ispagna son
gia mille e tre.)** You yearn for an equal, a woman of
power – yet you deny me the power that loving faithfully would afford me: that dress with its wide skirt
like a bell, its fichus, its form, its rapture of mischief . . .

---

* And in Spain already a thousand and three.

. . . No, I say, don't come tonight, and with a flick of the tongue I make absence, violently. And I'll be silent, too, Tadeusz, silent as Turandot with her murderous laws, withdrawn, cold as the moon. No longer a woman whose song of suffering cascades for you, chromatic, sliding, ascending or descending in imperceptible intervals, but a woman who understands that power resides in absence, in denial. No, I say, like Carmen, who knew how to drive men wild by refusals.

But no sooner are the words out of my mouth, Tadeusz, than everything changes. Once again you are a figure in a dream I'm having and you are tender and strong (suddenly Don Ottavio), and not perverse at all. You move seamlessly in time, retreating, easing yourself below me so that your body will obscure my view of the drop. (To go down, after all, is often as perilous as to go up.) Sure-footed, withstanding the sharp grass blades, the whirlwinds of my nerves, the fright which films my eyes, the showers of pebbles which, dislodged by my uncertain feet, whistle past you and vanish into the yawning space below us.

No, I say, don't come, and falling into the bathroom I pour out hot piss, tears: opera, as it were, without the redeeming form. Abjection, Tadeusz. The tree laying its bright eggs in the nest of the night.

Time passes by inches, Tadeusz. Dust falls from the air and gathers on the card table, on the phonograph, on the sideboard with its few faithless letters, on my mother's open hands. As in a dream I see my body spread out across your dark length like a pale horse,

bucking and flaring; this power, at least, I acknowledge. But still a dazzling fusillade of light pierces my
courage whenever men spit three times for luck, thinking that in this way they can cheat grief.

Sometimes, Tadeusz, I need you to take my hand.

Faithfully Yours

JANE DELYNN

Although I have long acknowledged, at least to myself, that I don't live for pleasure, it is only recently that I have been forced to admit that the mental tortures of regret and recrimination lie so profoundly at the core of my being. Perhaps, even, *are* the core of my being. I will tell you, in brief, how this realisation came to pass.

Picture a conference – you've been at one, I'm sure – filled with writers, or aspirants thereto, of the American variety, fiercely competitive, rabidly jealous, anxious both to secure a piece of the decreasingly sized pie for themselves and to prevent it from reaching the mouths of others. There are two thousand of us, or more, in a hotel in Boston, which is both a city and the dream of a city – a colonial city of the British Empire, horizontal, with parks and low skyline – a city where the taxi drivers still speak English and know how to get you where you are going. The skin of the people is white. Not an American city, after all.

There is a price for all good things, which in Boston takes the form of outrageous taxi fares.

I paid the driver and walked into the hotel. Stuffing the receipt into my pocket as I went through the revolving doors my attention was somewhat divided, so that I emerged almost stepping on to a soft carry-all someone had deposited right in front of the door. I was about to say something snotty to the boy in the baseball cap who was bending over to pick the bag up by the strap, when I realised it was not a boy but a woman. She was wearing jeans and a light brown leather jacket and her baseball cap was navy blue.

I was wearing a dark blue baseball-style cap myself, though mine was wool rather than cotton. My hair was shorter than hers, and my height lesser, and my age greater. I watched her walk to the elevator, where she joined a group of people, one of whom was doing her best to look like a man, though she was really too short to pull it off.

From the back, I realised her hair was long. She looked nothing like a boy.

I believe I've neglected to mention that it was not just any ordinary writers' conference, but the Perverse Writers' Conference. All writers' conferences are boring in their way, but the Perverse Writers' Conference perhaps less so than any other, for there is sure to be a very oversized man wearing rollerskates, and a very short woman who insists on smoking a cigar, and a whole host of people who are furious because the Physically Abundant have not been provided with extra-large seats, and that perfume (so distressing to the Allergically Impaired!) is not absolutely proscribed. Even our tee-shirts – 'I Lost It at the Movies' (Pee Wee Herman whacking off); '10 Things a Man Can do Better than a Woman (Rape You, Beat You, Give You VD, Forget to Pay Child Support . . .)'; 'Anything Worth Doing Is Worth Doing Badly' (two bored-looking women doing the

Unimaginable) – are superior. We are talking, in short, about the kind of a group where the only people likely to be found in the health club are women.

My bag was light so I managed to carry it to my room. It was a big room with two beds, perhaps too big: the television was so far away you would have had to sit at the little round breakfast table to see it. The radio was part of the television system and you could not turn it on from the bed. The bathroom had a hair drier (which I had brought) and many towels, but no shower cap, shoe horn, shoe polish, body lotion, cream rinse, telephone, or complimentary robe (none of which I had brought).

Before taking a shower I called room service. After a long and unsatisfactory discussion about available decaffeinated and herbal teas I ordered some hot water and lemon. Then I lay down in the water to take a long, skin-drying bath (there were no bath-oil beads or bubble bath either). The skin on my fingers would shrivel into lizards, but what did it matter? No one would care but me, and I didn't count.

Why didn't I 'count'? I have been pondering this my entire life and still have not found a satisfactory answer.

The door knock came as I was still ruminating. Hurriedly I pulled on a clean shirt (it got wet) and, with a towel around my waist, answered the door.

But it was not room service. It was my friend Barbara, who had the room next door. 'You weren't answering your phone,' she accused me.

'I'm taking a bath. Where have you been?' She raised her forearm so it was at a right angle to her upper arm and tensed her extraordinarily large bicep.

I settled back in my bath. Barbara turned on the TV and continued her post-workout stretch. The sound of college

basketball played pleasantly in the background while I tried to
space out. It seemed much safer to do this with Barbara in the
next room than it had been when I was alone. It is often more
enjoyable, if less exciting, to be with someone one is not in the
least attracted to. When the knock came and I heard Barbara's
voice asking 'Who is it?' I suddenly thought: what if room
service pulls out a gun and shoots her? I shivered. (Of course, for
I was in the now lukewarm water.) Barbara brought me in some
tea and I drank it in the bath, but despite the warm liquid inside
and outside (I turned the hot water on again) something in me
was still cold.

As I was trying to figure out what to wear, the phone rang. It
was my lover. Whereas an ordinary lover would have called to
say she missed me, or hoped I liked my room, or was having a
good time, my lover was calling to tell me how happy she was to
have the apartment to herself, the cat to herself, the kitchen to
herself, the sofa and bed to herself, the VCR and the three movies
she was planning to glom out on to herself.

I told her that I suspected much of her pleasure was in
informing me of this.

She laughed, and asked if I was having a good time.

'Not yet,' I said, 'but I think I will.'

'So the women are beautiful?'

'One is,' I said.

She told me she was going to shut off the answering machine
when she began her movie orgy. Therefore if I called her and
didn't get an answer I should not get paranoid.

I instantly got paranoid. To make myself feel better, I went
into specifics about the person in the baseball cap.

'Have a good time,' she said. As always, she sounded like she
meant it.

I had, of course, considered being unfaithful to my lover, and to that end had brought along my sexy underwear. To whom, at a conference of the Perverse, would such an idea not occur? My lover and I had had many illuminating and enlivening discussions on said topic, without ever having been able to come to a definitive answer. Almost anything I discuss with my lover gives rise to an illuminating and enlivening discussion, as she is vocal, intelligent and perverse – not just in the sexual sense but every way. I say this not out of partiality but in the interests of veracity. Indeed, I am not at all sure that the ability to discuss subjects interestingly and intelligently is a positive attribute for a relationship. (Certainly it is not something I ordinarily value – indeed, it is something I have often gone out of my way to avoid. Amongst other things, it is often extraordinarily fatiguing.)

What we came up with was this: fidelity was certainly impossible – in the theoretical sense – but unfortunately infidelity, though Platonically desirable (indeed, how could one find love in the midst of a relationship save through infidelity?), often foundered in practice, due to various weaknesses and fallacies of the human psyche, contingencies that even we ourselves (however superior we considered ourselves to be) might on occasion find ourselves prey to. We therefore assumed, in the contingent sense, an unarticulated but mutually observed discretion, and, in the Platonic sense, an only partly ironic expectation of the 'worst' – which, in the context of our peculiar relationship, might be the 'best' – as this assumption seemed to prolong the intensity of our sex life beyond what might reasonably have been expected.

I do not attempt to defend our peculiar relationship. All I can say, by way of exculpation, is our perverseness has less to do with choice of sexual object than with a shared infatuation for contradiction, complication, and other allures of the enigmatic and obscure.

One might go so far to say that, whereas in most relationships sex commences where the rational ends, in our relationship it is the sex that is rational and the conversation where the truly 'perverse' commences.

The idea that my lover was happy because I was away perked me up (as no doubt she had intended it should), and with this renewed confidence I was of course able to choose what, for that moment in time and the current state of my hair and skin and mood, was the 'perfect' thing to wear.

Overhearing all this, and observing my mood shift, Barbara assured me I was crazy.

But in her room, watching her change out of her sweatsuit into something if not much dressier then at least cleaner, overhearing her half of her conversation with her lover Lucinda (rather, *ode*, for surely its forms are as codified as any sonnet's, replete with 'me toos' and 'I miss you toos' and little smacks of the lips at the end), it struck me that it was Barbara's relationship (and not mine) that was crazy.

I am not sure when it became impossible to be 'natural' but probably sometime before it became *de rigueur* for people like us to wear baseball caps.

As it turned out, Lucinda hadn't come to Boston, not for honest perverse reasons, like my lover, but because she had a sore throat. Lucinda always had a sore throat when Barbara did her thing.

The cocktail party was large. The cocktail party was noisy. The cocktail party was filled with people drinking club soda fogged up with little squirtings of lime. It looked like abstinence but it was really the far side of indulgence, and I felt like a child with my silly wine spritzer.

The baseball caps were gone, replaced by dresses or man-styled suits – for the distaff side of the room. Some of the 'real' men wore jackets, but many just wore sport shirts and pants, or even tee-shirts and Levis. If someone had really short hair, the odds were at least even that it was a woman rather than a man.

I was amused to see that some blacks were still wearing dashiki-type outfits, and that a certain kind of woman dressed as boringly as she might have in the late 1970s, to prove that a certain kind of 'seriousness' will never go completely out of style.

I said hello to the woman whom I had been unfaithful to my lover with at the last Perverse Writers' Conference. It had not been a wholly satisfactory experience, at least in retrospect, because once my lover told me she did not find her attractive I realised I didn't find her attractive either.

We kissed each other on the cheek and told each other how well we looked. In fact, she did look well, mostly due to a little slip of a cocktail dress she was wearing, very unlike the wool pants she had worn last year. I realised my outfit (black stretch pants, fake leopard boots, black jacket) could have been one I wore last year (in fact, very likely *was* the one I had worn last year), and my confidence immediately evaporated.

The rest of the evening I spent trying, like everybody else, to find people who would tell me how great I looked and what a wonderful writer I was.

I looked for the woman in the baseball cap. Either I could not recognise her without her cap, or she was not there. I did see her short fat friend. But then I saw there were other short fat women around the room, and the more I looked the more I did not know which of them was the right short fat woman.

A normal person would have come to the conclusion that if you could not recognise someone without her baseball cap she could not be that attractive to you. But the way I looked at it was: it was my duty to uncover and recapture the mysterious kernel of attractiveness that had been kindled by the iconographic use of my favourite (at least to read about) sport.

I continued to search for the woman in the baseball cap all the next day – walking out of panels in the middle and catching only the final minutes of others, looking for that telltale headgear in the back of rooms or at the entrance to others. Even while I gave my own little speech my eyes anxiously kept working the room.

In this state of mind, of course, it was impossible to pay attention to the conference.

It was how I always acted when I had a crush on someone. Barbara kept telling me how stupid it was, but, as usual, I found it somehow 'witty'. It was all I could do not to call my lover and tell her about this. She was the only person in the world who would have understood.

No matter the state of your heart, it behooves you to eat dinner. I had been pestering Barbara to go someplace expensive and exotic to eat, but she wanted to hang around the hotel with some people she had run into earlier.

'Oh, all right,' I said grouchily. I was sleepy, sick of everybody. Or maybe it was just a sugar depletion fit. I kept flipping the plastic pages of the three-ring looseleaf tourist book the hotel had provided with brochures of various places to go to eat and things to see, without being able to come to a decision.

'Come on,' said Barbara.

She wore a jacket of denim over a vest of denim over a shirt of denim. For some reason it made her look more femme than when she wore a skirt. Watching her as she tied, with admirable lack of indecisiveness, a red bandanna around her neck, I grew more and more nervous about who I was, particularly in relation to the question of lipstick. I went into my room, smooshed on some make-up and gel, and put on a cowboy shirt.

It looked terrible, though last year it was great. I put on a black GAP tee-shirt, but I felt like an older person trying to imitate a twenty year old, so I took it off. I put on a silk shirt over the same stretch pants I wore the night before.

'What are you doing?' asked Barbara.

'Trying to get dressed.'

'You're fine. Come on.'

'I'm not fine.' But there was nothing left except a little black mini-skirt which my lover had insisted on slipping into my valise, and which I certainly could not put on so early in the evening (and most likely not at all), so I followed Barbara to the lobby. With every step I took I felt, for some reason, more and more like a transvestite.

Sitting with the people Barbara had arranged to meet for dinner was the woman in the baseball cap and her friend who looked like a man. I was happy they were there, and unhappy because of the silk shirt.

I placed myself opposite the woman in the baseball cap and ordered a burger, not so much because I wanted one as to show I was not 'politically correct' and would still eat meat.

Barbara's friends were discussing 'butchness' and 'femmeness'. The woman who looked like a man had come up with a series of categories into which all women – at least all women like us – could be divided. According to her theory, there were fourteen different ways of being a 'butch', and fourteen different ways of being a 'femme'. Certain kinds of butches would appeal to certain kinds of femmes, and vice versa, but other kinds were a 'must to avoid', kind of like a horoscope.

The different categories seemed to be determined not, as I had always thought, by how you were in bed, but by your haircut, your clothing, the way you walked and talked and came on to people in a bar.

The more she said the more nervous I got, and the more self-conscious about my silk blouse.

'That's all arbitrary,' I said. 'I often force myself to do things differently than I used to.'

Ah yes, she said, you could do that. But you could never really fool anybody. Because underneath your actions and your speech and your make-up and your clothing, there was something instinctive and unchangeable: for instance, the way you organised the different parts of your body, or where you held your hands when you weren't doing anything in particular with them. Just as, despite my gold earrings and my silk blouse and my fancy shoes, anybody could tell I was butch. Even if I wore high heels and a skirt, I was butch.

'But I'm passive in bed,' I said. Everybody laughed.

Everybody was staring at me. My hands were on my hips. Embarrassed, I took them from my hips and placed them on my lap. Then I became embarrassed about being embarrassed, and tried to sneak them back on my hips.

'You see,' she said, 'you can't help that.'

'Yes I can.' But a little later I caught myself with my hands on my hips again.

I leaned forward and began eating the pretzels on the table, just to have something to do with my hands. I finished several bowls before the food arrived. The burger was thick and difficult to eat; the lettuce and tomato kept falling out, and occasionally a glop of ketchup. The others were all eating vegetarian cheese or yogurt-type things. They finished before I did, then sat there calmly, apparently unworried about what to do with their hands when they weren't eating.

But whoever we were and regardless of where on the appearance dialectic we made our stand, we all listened intently to our man-tailored philosopher. And the difference that began to seem truly significant was not whether we wore jeans or skirts, silk blouse or tee-shirt, but that we were having the conversation at all. What seemed truly alien was the waitress, whose every gesture signified innocence and unself-consciousness – despite the fact that she was wearing too bright red lipstick and an outfit that, with its short skirt and low-cut top, surely was meant to be 'sexy' (although I doubt whether any one of us would have found it so). You could only get away with dressing like that if you did it with the proper degree of irony. But the waitress was so unironical she did not seem to notice any of us as being 'different' from her.

As she took away our plates, the woman who dressed like a man (her name was 'Connie', but her girlfriend called her 'Con') again began talking about femmes, but the waitress did not hear.

Or if she heard, she did not react.

Or if she reacted, it was not visible.

Perhaps, after all, a waitress (or a waiter), can never be visible. And that is why it is often so difficult to remember which one is yours when you want your check.

Meanwhile the woman in the baseball cap said very little, her only sign of nervousness the cigarette she suddenly asked Connie to light.

When she inhaled the bottom of her nostrils flared, and I felt I was watching a 1940s movie in which the detective finds himself in love with a girl who pretends she is in love with him but is more likely just leading him on.

'I didn't know you'd gone back to smoking,' Connie said.

'Just for this weekend,' she replied, 'or Roberta will kill me.' She glanced up and saw me looking at her, then turned her head away. In profile, I saw the line that demarcated the part of the visual universe that was her face from the part of the visual universe that was the background glowing with a soft white light, presumably from a light source behind her head. A cloud of white formed out of the two funnels of white she blew from her nostrils and dissolved upwards in the air. I may have been deceived, but it seemed she was doing it all for me.

Because it was suddenly OK for me, despite whatever I wore, to be butch, because I suddenly knew, despite the baseball cap, she was a femme, I smiled my slit-eyed smile at her, the one you see on my book jackets, the sleepy-looking one that is both natural and artificial. It was directed first at her eyes, then at her breasts, then I ostentatiously moved them further down to where the edge of the table cut off the rest of her body.

'Are you going to the dance tonight?' she asked.

'Yes.'

'Are you wearing what you're wearing?'

'No.'

Due to my evident confusions, Connie suggested coming to my room and dressing me. I tried on all my outfits, including the little black mini-skirt. Under her gaze, my clothing no longer seemed ambiguous and subtle, but a sign of cowardice and confusion.

Looking at myself as an object of desire rather than as the one desiring, I wondered which of the fourteen types of butches – the ones who were tomboys and the ones who were punks, the ones who were 'daddies' and the ones who were faggots, the ones who were 'mamma's boys' and the ones who were jocks, the ones who were cowboys and the ones who were sluts, the ones who were 'stone butches' and the ones who masqueraded as femmes, and all the other kinds I could not remember – I was, but I could not tell.

Although I had worn my black jeans on the train and did not consider them 'dressy' enough for the dance, Connie insisted I wear them. She kind of liked the man's shirt I had brought to wear under a Perry Como-esque sweater the next day, but she said it needed something else to make it dressier – like a tie.

'I don't have a tie.'

'I do.'

She told me to leave my pocketbook behind, and stick my money and the plastic card that took the place of a room key in my shoe. Sometime in the past I had done this, perhaps in high school, following a sweaty-palmed boy on to the dance floor. Going to her room I felt the excitement I had then, of pretending to be something I was not, even though what I was pretending to be, this time, was myself.

Connie changed out of the suit she was wearing into another, equally masculine one, but of somewhat lighter material. She took a shirt off a hanger in the closet. It looked exactly like a man's, but it had been tailormade especially for her, because her neck and wrist length and breasts made it impossible for her to wear a man's shirt off the rack. The shirt had black and gold studs instead of buttons, and cufflinks to match.

I fingered these. They felt substantial and real, part of the same world in which I hid my money in my shoe. Once I bought my father cufflinks. I used to like looking at them in the little box which was not just a box but a kind of home for them – in the sense a cat box is a home – with its little padded throne covered in a kind of fuzzy bluish-grey material. That kind of jewellery seemed so much more real and intelligent than my mother's. But now cufflinks and suspenders seemed anachronisms no longer worn by men, but only by women such as me.

Instead of putting on her shirt, she handed it to me.

'I can't wear this,' I said.

'Why not?'

'It's too nice. What if I spill something on it?' She looked at me. 'It's just not me,' I said.

'It *is* you. You don't really think silk shirts are you, do you?'

I put the shirt on. Then Connie lay several ties around my neck, to see which worked best with the shirt and my skin colouring. We settled on a black-on-grey silk one. It felt substantial too, and real.

It was me, of course, and it was my father. And she was my mother as well as my father as she knotted the tie around my neck.

Then Connie's girlfriend Sandy came into the room and told Connie how great I looked, and that Elaine (the woman in the baseball cap) would be sure to think so too.

I felt like a man overhearing female gossip.

Connie made me brush my hair to get rid of the gel, then rubbed some shiny man's hair cream on it, so that it was slicked back like a 1940s gangster, or Pat Riley. Usually when my hairdresser did stuff with my hair I felt as if she were trying to make me into something I was not, but Connie seemed to be bringing out the essence of who I was. As to whether or not I liked this person, I was not sure. She finished it off with a dab of 'Brut'.

I looked at myself in the mirror. In it was a woman who was clearly a woman, but a woman who was attempting to get at something that was the essence of a man. Perhaps because it was false it seemed more like a 'man' than a 'real' man did.

Back in the lobby it took me a few seconds to recognise Elaine. She was wearing a silvery latex mini-skirt and matching top through which the curves of her ribs and the convexity and concavity of her chest when she breathed were visible.

'How did you get it on?' I asked.

'Talcum powder.'

I had never seen latex in any colour but black or red or green before. The silver shimmered softly, reflecting the hotel lights like an inviting pool you might fall into. On her head she wore a black hat with little dot conglomerates stuck here and there on the veil. My mother had worn hats like this once, but I hadn't seen one, outside of the movies, in decades.

Connie's girlfriend wore a black tube dress. Other women surrounded Barbara and Connie and me in their mini-skirts, their spandex jumpsuits, their lingerie tops, women who in the day looked just like me. It was like discovering a new world, but one that existed not instead of but behind the old one. This made the old one seem not less but more interesting.

Those women looked at Connie and me, too, as if we were concealing a mystery, one that had to do not just with studs and cufflinks and ties and the smell of man's cologne, but something stranger and sexier. I could see it in their eyes. I had the power.

I wanted the power. I wanted them to swoon at my fucking

feet. I wanted to be the heterosexual male rapist. I wanted to be a faggot and have them suck my cock.

'Shall we dance?'

I led Elaine, in her strange little veiled hat, on to the dance floor.

You know how people dance: they stand apart, they shift their legs, they tilt their heads from one side to the other, they snap their fingers, they rotate around themselves like the moon, they revolve in circles around an imaginary centre located somewhere between themselves and their partner.

Every time I revolved back to a certain spot, I saw Barbara looking at me. I knew what she was thinking: I was a phony, not a real butch at all. But I was doing as well as if I were a real butch.

I stopped to buy Elaine and Connie's girlfriend a beer. Then Connie bought me a beer. Barbara wasn't drinking.

Elaine stood talking to me. The veil hung so far down that she had to slip the bottle under it to drink. The veil hung between the bottle and me, and I yearned to push it away.

We talked as we drank, and though she looked at other people, she stayed with me. She told me about her life in the small town in which she lived on the other side of the continent, with children she had had in an earlier life, and the woman she lived with now, and the ways in which it was good and the ways in which it was not. And the more she talked the more vivid that far-off life in California became, and the less vivid this real life in Boston. And as her life in California became more vivid, so did my own life in New York, until I knew that if we did not start dancing soon it would be too late.

I knew that if she would dance with me again, she would sleep with me. I put my hand, lightly, on her right hip, as I led her to the dance floor. Ever so subtly, she leaned her hip into my hand. But when we reached the dance floor, she began to move away, into that solitary dance where we rotate and revolve around ourselves.

It wasn't me. For years I had forgotten, but the shirt and tie made me remember – even if, years ago, it had been someone else wearing them. I pulled Elaine to me, and with my right hand on her left hip, and my left hand holding her right, I began to lead her in a version of a dance you call the lindy.

I drew her towards me. I pushed her away; I spun her around under my arm, one way and then the other; we put our left arms behind our heads and slipped away from each other till our hands caught; face to face we held hands and brought them up and over our heads and, still holding hands, rotated under them; we danced side by side, my left arm around her; and we danced with my front to her back, in sync.

It seemed like the real dancing, the dancing I had done in high school, before people stopped dancing with each other and started dancing with themselves. Only then I had been the one being led, and not the one leading.

But the leading came naturally, like the shiny hair goo and cufflinks and tie.

And when we were not doing any of the above, I held her left hip next to my right one, and with my left hand on her right, twirled her around and around in circles that were both rotations and revolutions, faster and faster so that I became a fifteenth kind of butch, a Fred Astaire kind of butch, and the people around us stopped dancing, stood in a circle, and clapped.

It was my finest hour. When you are a Fred Astaire kind of butch you can have anything you want, and you should.

I looked for Barbara. She was gone.

The lights were wrong. They wouldn't dim. The one by the bed was the least bright, but it was magnified by its reflection in the mirror over the dresser so that if you were lying on the bed it glared in your eyes. The light on the dresser was brighter but further away and because of the lampshade didn't reflect in the mirror. I opened the bathroom door a little, but the lights were fluorescent. There was a hanging lamp over the little table where I ate my room service breakfast, but lying on the bed you could see the bulb underneath the shade.

The furniture was dark, shiny, the top covered in a Formica pattern of imitation wood. The people who invent this stuff, the people who market this stuff, and the people who buy it for hotels have done a vast disservice to millions of people all over the globe by insulting their eyes and their brains.

Elaine had refused to accompany me to my room, but told me she would sneak up after she had said good night to Connie and Sandy. For the sake of the lover back home in California, she was maintaining the appearance of fidelity.

For the sake of my lover in New York, I did not want to maintain the appearance of fidelity, and this upset me.

I took off my shoes and lay down on the bed. But I did not want to pull the covers off the bed, and the bedspread, shiny and quilted, was cold and slippery. I stood up, smoothed out the bedspread, walked over to the little breakfast table.

I felt short, very un-Fred Astaire, without my shoes, so I put them back on.

I fiddled with the radio stations. It was not New York. I could not find what I wanted. I settled for some 1970s music. Once offensive and jolting, it was now played on the 'soft rock' station.

What could I do while I waited? A book or television would alter who I was at this moment. I did not want this, as Elaine liked who I was at this moment. Then it occurred to me: if I were to read my own book, I would only become more of who I was.

But when I got it out and looked at it, the words I had written, about a character who was me, seemed to have nothing to do with me. I remembered writing the words, but not the feelings.

I looked up the hotel movie guide, and ordered something from the 'adult' channel.

These movies are all alike. Women stroking each other in that soft way that is the only way men can imagine women have sex, and a man watching, waiting to reap the results of all this preparation.

I unzipped my jeans and began to touch myself, but I'm not sure if I was actually turned on, or just trying to be turned on. I took off my shirt. It might be interesting if I answered the door naked, except for the tie, as might happen in a porno movie. But my stomach looked big in the mirror, not butch at all, and the breasts seemed to contradict the iconography of the tie. I buttoned up my jeans and put the shirt back on, but left it open, my breasts half visible, the tie hanging loosely down over my collar.

Fifteen, twenty minutes went by. The phone rang. There it is, I thought, she's not coming. I felt both angry and relieved.

But she had only forgotten my room number.

Before Elaine entered the room, she took the 'DO NOT DISTURB' sign from the inside knob and put it on the outside. 'Of course, Connie and Sandy figured out what I was doing,' she said.

I wanted to kiss her, but instead I said, 'The lights are fucked.'

She got a towel from the bathroom and put it over the lamp, so the glow was diffused.

'How'd you know that?' I asked.

'I've made love in hotel rooms before.'

She looked at the TV a minute and said she had watched that movie the previous night, then she lowered the sound. She took off her shoes, then her hat and her veil. I will not insult you by telling you the irrelevant colour of her eyes. It was too dark to see anything in them.

'I want to kiss you,' she said.

I had brushed my teeth, of course, but the beer was still in my mouth. As I opened my mouth, as I stuck out my tongue, as I let her tongue brush the inside of my mouth, I was conscious of this.

I was so conscious of the taste of beer in my mouth I wasn't conscious of the taste in her mouth, not even whether there was toothpaste or not.

Our mouths went towards each other. We were standing. We did what we were supposed to do. Then, awkwardly, I pulled her on top of me onto the bed.

I looked over to the movie. A man was entering a woman, from behind.

With her on top of me, I became confused. Was I supposed to be a man or a woman?

I put my mouth on hers. I knew where it was supposed to start. I knew where it was supposed to go. I knew what I was supposed to feel.

'I love you' went through my mind, though of course I did not mean it. Lately for some reason, I had been unable to feel desire without these words parading through my mind.

My lover's image was in my head. I pictured myself in bed with her, telling her about this night. She would be turned on, by the dancing and the latex outfit and the hat.

'You seem far away,' Elaine said.

'No.'

'I can feel it.'

'That kind of remark only makes me further away.'

I kissed her again, but she wouldn't open her mouth. In my head I saw how a man did it, unbuckling the belt, unzipping the pants, slipping the fingers up the skirt.

If I opened my eyes I would surely see some similar movie scene, without having to invent it. But that seemed more difficult somehow.

'Tell me what you're thinking about,' she said.

'I can't.'

If she had been my lover I would have told her, and the thoughts that were going through my mind would have amused and excited her. But I did not trust her to be amused and excited. I felt she would get angry and leave the room.

She moved off me. She lay on her side next to me. I propped my head on my elbow and looked at her. She was very attractive, more attractive probably than my lover.

I felt that to kiss her, to really kiss her, I would have to open myself up in a way that would erase my lover from my mind.

'I really like the way you look,' I said. I traced the outline of her lips and her nose with my finger. People did this in movies. But still, I was not turned on.

We tried to kiss again, then we lay there awhile. I shut my eyes, and fell asleep for a tiny part of a second. Her words woke me. 'Maybe this isn't such a hot idea.' I giggled, at the word 'hot'. 'What are you laughing at?' she asked.

'That word.' She looked puzzled. 'Hot.' She didn't laugh. I wasn't sure whether it was because she didn't understand or because she didn't approve. 'You're probably right,' I said. I felt bad, and wanted to do something to make her stay. But in order to make her want to stay I had to do the thing that was the reason

I wanted her to stay, and this was what, despite my conscious inclination, I was unable to do.

'Are you often like this?' she asked.

'No.' This was true, although it seemed like it could have been, in fact should have been, a lie, and that it was only by chance it wasn't. My lover would have understood.

I did not want to make love with my lover either, but grow sleepy talking to her.

I thought about talking about all this to Elaine, but it seemed too complicated. My perversities might be able to charm a person of leisure, a person without children, but not a person of responsibility, a mother.

'Why don't we just go to sleep,' she said. 'Maybe we'll feel better in the morning.'

I watched her get undressed. Like a mother, she folded her clothing responsibly, whereas I flung mine on a chair. We both left our underpants on. There was a terrible silence after the TV was turned off.

As scared as I am of desire, I'm scared of the lack of desire more.

In the dark it would be all right. In the dark, where no one could see anything, the tendrils on my arm would surely wake themselves from their embarrassed slumber and tremble to desires once forbidden. In the dark, under the surface of my actions and my speech and my make-up and my clothing, where no one could see the way I organised the different parts of my body when I was not doing anything in particular with them, would not my hands, my feet, my breasts, do what, in days gone by, they had always done?

Of course, with the shirt and tie off, I was a different person than the one she had liked.

I put my arm around her. She turned away, so I was hugging her back. I moved my hands up to her breast, but her arms guarded them. 'Shh,' she said, though I had not said anything.

Almost always I have trouble sleeping. The window of opportunity is small, the distractions great, the consciousness of the difficulty involved the greatest hazard of all. I thought about all the other times I had lain in bed, unable to listen to the radio or TV or turn on a light to read, next to women who were somehow able to breathe deeply and sonorously, even after a scene like the one Elaine and I had just had. Usually they were what is referred to as 'normal'. As suspect as my motivation is, so is theirs.

The longer I thought about it, the angrier I got. After about twenty minutes or so, I realised my pants were wet.

I put my hand on Elaine's shoulder. 'Could you put your hand inside me?' I asked.

She shook me off, but I repeated the question.

She rolled over. 'Could you put your hand inside me, just for a few minutes?' I repeated. She sat up and turned on the light. She looked at me as if I were some vaguely repugnant object. Then she swung her legs from under the sheets to the carpet.

I sat on the side of the bed watching her as she got dressed. I had no talcum powder and it took her quite a while to shimmy the latex back on.

She put on her shoes then walked to the door. 'I'm sorry,' she said.

'I'm sorry too.' I felt empty and sad, as if it were a long relationship that was ending.

I left the door open till she turned the corner. First I took the 'DO NOT DISTURB' sign off the knob, then I put it back.

I couldn't sleep. I never can when I drink. I took aspirin, vitamin

C, water. Elaine's face never left my mind. I'd been unable to have sex with her because I kept thinking of my lover, and now I was unable to sleep because I kept thinking of Elaine. I would think of her, I knew, the next night in New York, when I lay in bed next to my lover and tried to have sex with her.

In the past I have always had the conviction, that what I was doing with a woman in a room was the most important thing in the entire world. My mind still had this conviction, but not my body.

I yearned to call my lover to discuss why this was no longer the most important thing in the world, and also what was, but the phone machine would not be turned on for many hours.

We had arranged to meet at ten for breakfast. I'd liked the idea of showing up for breakfast with Elaine on my arm, sleepy-eyed and satisfied. As it was, I went downstairs with Barbara. She seemed unduly pleased by my recounting of my failure.

Elaine was already at the table, a little pot of *espresso* before her. She made room for me next to her, and we politely kissed each other on the cheek. Barbara looked at us as if there was something the matter with us.

'What happened to your baseball cap?' I asked. It was the first time I had seen her in public without something on her head.

'It was Connie's. I gave it back before I forgot.'

So she, too, had been dressed by Connie. We were, both of us, imposters. It made me both like her more and feel less attracted.

In between bites of toast and eggs, we discussed what had (not) happened. Despite my contempt for people who live in northern California I decided to try to do this. 'Sometimes I have trouble responding when I'm supposed to,' I said. 'I keep having these conversations in my head with my girlfriend. Maybe I should have told you. Also, I felt you only liked me because I was wearing Connie's shirt.'

She looked at me as if I were crazy. 'Who likes people because of what they're wearing?'

'I do,' I admitted.

'You mean, you liked *me* because of my latex outfit?'

'Don't forget the cigarette,' I added.

It wasn't the truth – at least not entirely – but I wanted her to think it was, so she'd get angry, so I could apologise, even if what I was really sorry about was something else.

Of course, even as we were talking, I was having another conversation in my head, with my girlfriend. It seemed a much more interesting conversation than the one I was actually having, and yet all I was doing was reciting to her the details of my conversation with Elaine.

Connie and her girlfriend arrived. I was hoping Elaine hadn't yet spoken with them, but immediately they started in with the jokes. At first it bothered me, then as I drank more coffee I began to find it amusing, for the more they talked the less and less Elaine and I were who we were and the more we became these characters in a story, a somewhat perverse comedy of manners whose subtext was subtle and complex without being in the least pathological, which partook nothing of abuse or incest or any of the other generic explanations about people like us. The 'me' character in this story was provocative, ironical and enigmatic, and although I happen to consider myself provocative, ironical and enigmatic, my character in this story seemed to embody those characteristics in a wholly different manner than the way I thought I did.

It was kind of like high school, where you spend all your time talking about your friends, but if so at least I was in the 'in' group, and I decided it was OK. Better than OK. 'Fun.'

When I said goodbye I kissed Sandy first, then Connie. I had planned an extraordinary gesture for Elaine, a Fred Astaire kind of grasping and swooping backward, but she must have thought I was going to skip her entirely, for she pulled me toward her as I was still moving away from Connie, so I had no time to prepare my histrionic kiss, and had to give her an ordinary one instead.

It began to snow before we left the station. First it was late afternoon, then it was twilight, then it was night. It reminded me of something . . . good . . . long ago, on the train with the snow coming down, Barbara and I and the others in our comfortable seats speeding past the towns of Rhode Island and Connecticut where normal people lived. I wanted to be them, for a week, maybe. No. Less. For the length of a movie of their lives.

The soundtrack, against the snow and the houses and the stations and my face reflected in the window as it grew darker, was a conversation with Elaine and my lover, as overheard by Barbara. I was explaining myself to them, first my desire to feel, then my fear of that desire and how that fear made it impossible for me to feel, then my embarrassment about all this, my desire to have this understood and forgiven and, most of all, be loved in spite of it, which was surely the greatest desire of all, as well as my only hope of salvation.

Elaine and Barbara and my lover looked at me as I talked – the me who was not just 'me' but a character in Connie's story – and the houses sped by and the snowflakes got bigger and the sky grew darker and my face was reflected ever brighter in the glass, and as I spoke my voice grew softer and softer until my lovers and friends fell under the spell of my words. And as long as I kept talking I knew I could have them all, *for ever* (and anyone else, of course), and the more I realised this the more I was able to feel – by which I mean my pants got wet – and I became a normal person, just like you.

✥ *The Space Generator*

SCOTT BRADFIELD

Audrey said simply, 'I'm not saying I *hate* my husband, Sarah, I'm just saying I can't stand having him *around*. I think there's a big difference between *hating* someone and just needing, well, a little va*ca*tion from them every now and again.'

Across the green Formica table, Sarah raised her coffee cup and sniffed. Something darted behind her green eyes, like a fish in a bowl. She sniffed her coffee one more time, secretly watching Audrey.

'It's more like an allergy or something,' Audrey said. 'You know – like people who can't stand being around dogs or linen, or things like that. I still *love* Harry and all. I still respect him very much as an individual. I'm talking about something much deeper than the way I *feel* about Harry. It's not *emotional*, you see. It's *physical*, it's a simple matter of *physics*. It's like some microscopic spore, some secret radiation he gives off that irritates my skin. I don't know how else to explain it. I just get real nervous whenever Harry's around. I start to itch, my eyes water. Sometimes I even feel a little sick to my stomach. If I walk into the next room and close the door, I feel better – but only for a while. Then I can hear him, moving around the house. Or I can smell his body, like the smell of sour aftershave. I start to feel nervous again. It's like I don't belong in my own house any more. It's like I don't belong in my own bed.' Audrey reached for a damp dishcloth and wiped a stray bit of fried egg from the toaster. 'And now it's like I feel so *guilty* all the time . . . I mean, Harry's starting to resent sleeping on the couch every night, and I can't blame him really. I try to explain that it's just a phase I'm going through, just an allergy or something, and one of these days, before you know it, bang. I'll get over it.' Audrey was still holding the damp dishcloth. She gazed thinly at the shiny toaster.

Sarah put down her cup. Then she brushed some crumbs into her hand and shovelled them on to the saucer with a hard, succinct gesture, as if she were disposing of bad karma.

'I've been allergic to cat hair all my life,' Sarah said. She was looking straight at Audrey, but Audrey wasn't looking at her. 'It's not something that just comes and goes. Once you're allergic to something like cat hair, well, that's all there is to it. You're stuck with it the rest of your life.'

'Well, maybe.' Audrey was sitting at the table now, staring out the bright window at a dead tree in the garden. Flat, mushroom-like green and orange parasites blossomed up and down its grey trunk. The leaves were gone, the branches mulchy and twisted. Audrey thought it dimly funny that the orange and green parasites were far prettier than the tree itself had ever been. I'm not saying it's like a *real* allergy or anything, Sarah. I'm just using allergy as a sort of metaphor. I'm using allergy as a figure of speech.'

It was especially difficult whenever Harry tried to be sympathetic or understanding.

'Of *course* you don't understand what's happening to you, honey,' Harry said, precariously seated on the edge of the sofa. He leaned warmly into the upholstered spaces dividing them while Audrey sat watching her knees. Audrey was sitting on a small antique stuffed chair they had received as a wedding gift from Audrey's mother.

'The mind's an extraordinarily rare and complex organism,' Harry told her. 'I mean, if you under*stood* what your problem was, we'd have it solved by now. It wouldn't *be* a problem if we could *solve* it. Oh, Audrey.' At this point Harry threw up his arms with a long sigh of obstinate affection. 'I'm sure we'll straighten things out eventually. I just wish I could come over there right this minute and give you a really big hug.'

Usually Audrey cooked his dinner while he was at work and left it out on the kitchen table, sealed in a microwave-resistant Saran Wrap. She would print the minimal heating instructions on the back of torn envelopes and grocery coupons. Microwave MED two minutes, her notes said. I've turned in early. Love, Audrey. Then she went in and lay awake behind the locked door of their master bedroom. Every evening at seven fifteen she heard his car lift into the driveway, the suspension emitting its telltale, misaligned little screak. Tension accumulated as she heard him ascend the stairs and open the front door, as if his presence was being monitored by lists of enzymes in her stomach. The tension was nearly intolerable by the time Harry reached the kitchen. He began making cabinet doors slam and cutlery clatter. Audrey grew dizzy and lightheaded. The ceiling seemed to slant, and something trembled underneath her bed. This is Harry, she kept thinking to herself, over and over again. It's just Harry, he won't hurt you. There's no reason to be upset.

She could feel him verging out there, a diagram of weight and cool intention. Sometimes Harry sat down silently and ate his dinner. Other times, however, he uttered a rough, compensatory sigh, just loud enough for her to hear. On nights when Harry sighed, Audrey couldn't relax or fall asleep. Instead she went into the adjoining bathroom and took a valium, or vomited into the bleached and glistening white toilet bowl. Then she lay awake in bed, listening to Harry's eating or washing-up sounds. Harry taking off his pants and shirt. Harry brushing his teeth. Harry throwing spare sheets and blankets on to the couch and snapping off all the lights. Harry out there. Out there. Tonight, tomorrow, and the night after that.

'Let's try to remember that space is just an illusion, honey. All distances are relative. Between any two points lies an infinitude of other points, an immeasurable gulf of other spaces.' On especially terrible nights, Harry insisted they talk. While Audrey sat at one end of the couch, he sat at the other. 'I promise I won't touch you,' he assured her at the start. 'I promise I won't move any closer.'

While Harry talked, Audrey tried to concentrate on the microscopic. If she were the size of an atom, she would be hurtling through different notions of distance now, different illusions of space. But however hard she tried to concentrate on the soft indeterminate world of matter, all she could hear was Harry's voice. 'Relax,' he said. 'Talk things through. We're in no hurry. Whatever happens, I'll *always* understand.' It was as if even her own senses defined limits and conditions her skin could not accept, informing the atmosphere of these pale, museum-like spaces that intruded everywhere like light or energy. If she could vanish into the pocked, rocketing surfaces of particles, everything would be OK again. She wouldn't feel this weight and intention from his side of the couch.

'Are you *sure* you're all right?' he kept asking, over and over again, as if he liked the sound of his own voice. 'Are you *sure*? We won't rush things, we *won't* put any pressure on you. Are you *sure*? Are you *sure* you're all right?' His voice was following her down the long vertiginous hallway now, into the bathroom's bright latex glare. 'I really miss sleeping with you at night. I really miss everything we once had together.' That was Harry coming up behind her, hurrying, pulmonary, always warm and wanting, always trying to make her spaces his. She could smell and touch him, taste him, and some other sensation, like weight or humidity in the back of her mouth. If she tried, she could even look across the wide, bright room and see his flushed and sincere face smiling at her. Always smiling directly at her.

'What *was* that?' she asked, reaching for her glass of white wine. She was sitting on the couch again. The bath and bedroom both seemed very far away. 'I can't even remember any more, Harry. What *was* it we once had together? And why do we want it back?'

'Women are a whole lot spookier than men, that's all there is to it.' Harry was eating lunch with his sister Denise at the East Bay Deli in Santa Monica. On the phone he had promised Denise he wouldn't make any smart remarks about her new haircut. 'It's all that hormone stuff. Menstruating, lunar orbits, astrology, witchcraft and taboo. There's some sort of inalienable cosmic stuff in women, some secret metrics that never quite scan. Women's minds are filled with expectation and advantage, vacuum and verge, desire and oxygen. It's because women are always expecting something other than the ordinary, something more powerful and compelling than all the boring domestic stuff they already know. Women's minds are far too big to exist within the mere fizz and beep of our real and tiny world. What they've got's never quite good enough for them; what they want's always more than space and time can afford. Women expect strange and beautiful things to happen at every moment, even inside their own bodies, even inside the furthest places their own blood goes. Did I tell you I'm sleeping on the couch these days? I don't know – two, maybe three months now. I'm married and practically forty, and every night of the week I go home and sleep on the couch.'

Denise was eating an oleaginous meatball sandwich. Each time she lifted it to her mouth, oil splattered the corrugated white paper plate. She touched the corners of her mouth periodically with a scratchy white paper napkin.

'Maybe she's like going through some sort of midlife crisis, Harry, Maybe she's menopausal. Kind of like what happened to Mom.'

'Audrey's only thirty-two,' Harry said. They were sitting outside on the chilly patio, watching Lincoln Boulevard get busier with shiny cars and trucks. 'You don't go through menopause at thirty-two, Denise. And I don't care what you've been hearing on "Oprah"!'

'Some women do.' Denise's new hair was a bright, pinkish colour, and Harry tried not to look. 'Some women have PMT, Harry. Pre-menstrual tension. It lasts for weeks and weeks. Then, as soon as their first cycle ends, pow. It starts up all over again.'

It wasn't too long before Audrey dreaded being in the same house as Harry even when Harry wasn't there. Even when Harry was at work or visiting his family, it was as if their home contained some formal resonance, some remembered intimacy of dimension and geometry and wall. Harry's chair, Harry's couch, Harry's dirty dishes, Harry's warm and always muggy laundry. Harry-ness. Harriosity. Harryific.

'Harry is a very thoughtful, considerate man with hardly any chauvinistic tendencies whatsoever,' Audrey repeatedly told herself out loud, using her voice to fill the spaces around her with something that wasn't her husband. 'He is moderately handsome, and pays people all the polite and proper attentions. Some of my girlfriends even think he's sexy in a sort of funny unspecific way.' Sometimes Audrey stood alone in the middle of the living room, afraid to commit herself to furniture. She could feel the earth turning, the universe expanding, a blizzard of elementary particles bristling and wheeling around her neck and face like metaphysics. There are places within places, Audrey told herself. Between any two points resides an infinity of other points. Even when people are very close to you, they can still be a million miles away. And versa vice-uh.

'Harry is a considerate and thoughtful lover who always encourages me to be honest with my feelings.' Audrey was moving down the empty hallway, opening the doors of closets and cupboards, as if to reassure herself Harry wasn't hiding somewhere. 'Harry truly *cares* about me, and isn't like all those phony male types, you know, who go around pre*tend*ing they care, like they think they ought to.'

Sometimes she would stand in the middle of the living room, looking at the pale yellow lamplight distributed across things like a protectant, rehearsing her next conversation with Sarah. Other times, sensing the perilous spaces between things, she went to the kitchen telephone and called.

'It's like he's *scraping* at me, Sarah. Like I'm always being, what do they do to your skin when you're pockmarked? Like

I'm always being *abraded*. There's something metal about him, about the way he tastes. I can smell him in the house when he's not here. It's like he's always about to be here. It's like he's almost here already, even when he's nowhere to be found.'

Sarah said, 'Take a valium, honey. Take a valium and lie down for a while.'

'I think I've got to get away for a few days, a few weeks or something. But I keep thinking that if I go away, I won't come back. If I leave him now, I'll never have the courage to come back ever again.'

Audrey was starting to cry, and reached for a damp dish towel. I'm always crying these days, she thought. She didn't even understand the deep, formal ballistics of her own body any more.

Sarah's voice beat in the telephone receiver like electricity, spinning with warm chemical insurgency. 'Don't break down on me, Audrey. You're breaking down on me. Don't break down on me, honey. Don't leave me here all alone.'

'But if I don't go away, I'll never stop crying.' Audrey turned to look for the kitchen chair. It seemed infinitely far away, white oak and polished, material and severe. 'I'm always sick to my stomach, I never get any sleep. There's something wrong with me, Sarah, and I don't understand. There's something terribly wrong with me that I don't understand.'

Harry visited Audrey every day and sat beside her among the sagging green lawn chairs and sea-green grass.

'I think I'm starting to agree with your doctors on this one, baby.' He sat beside her and held her hand. Her hand felt cold and dry and utterly volitionless, like a magazine or a newspaper. 'We tried it *your* way and where did it get us? We gave you all the space you wanted, even when you wanted more space than you knew what to do with. Now you've gone and developed what the doctors call an irrational metaphysic. The brain's metaphysic is that ordering mechanism which is always trying to make the world it sees into a dream of what it wants to become. It's not that you hate *me*, Audrey; it's not *my* personal space you resent. It's just your wanting to be everywhere except where you are. You're not satisfied with *your*self as an individual, Audrey, and that's why you can't stand to be with *me*. It's a very complex and perfectly explainable series of phenomena which Dr Westmore understands perfectly. Leaving me will just make you worse, honey. You've got to learn to love me again in order to love yourself. Dr Westmore is a Laingian Buddhist and he respects your neuroses very much. He studied with R. D. Laing in Scotland, but he was originally born in Nepal.'

Meanwhile, Audrey sat in her lawn chair and gazed at the placid green grass. Green green. Thinking about the grass, she couldn't see Harry at all. She could barely even hear his voice across the wide green vault of space she tossed up between them whenever he was around. Space is something you make, Audrey thought. Voices are something you are.

'Anyway, honey. Relax and get well. That's the only job I want to see *you* doing for quite a while yet.'

Harry turned and saw the smiling nurse approach. The nurse was carrying a steel tray on which bright pills were apportioned by tiny white corrugated paper cups.

'Hello,' he said. 'I see it's already time for your medication.'

When Harry returned each evening to his house alone, he slept on the couch. It was as if the house expected it, as if his relationship with Audrey contravened mere facts like space and time. The closed bedroom door made him nervous, but he preferred it closed. He could still sense her presence brooding in there, listening to him eat his meals, growing more and more tense in the big bed. Her awareness filled the house with a stiff, simmering hesitancy. There was something planetary about it, defining invisible laws of attraction and repulsion, orbit and ellipse. He should not enter the bedroom. He should not linger overlong in the adjoining hall. He should sleep on the couch, and prepare his own breakfasts and dinners. In the morning, he should leave for work as quickly and quietly as possible.

His sense of time collapsed neatly and without resistance, like pop-up cardboard landscapes in a children's book. He came home and went to work. He bought groceries and dropped off laundry at the cleaner's. On weekends, he attended double-feature films at the shopping centre, where the minimal compact theatres resembled the leaning, gravity-padded chambers of jumbo passenger planes. Sometimes he cleaned. Whenever he entered the master bedroom, he carried the vacuum with him, or Formula 409 and a damp rag, as if he required a concrete alibi.

'Maybe you think I'm repulsive,' he told the empty room. 'But that doesn't mean I feel repulsive. Maybe it's not a psychological problem we're dealing with here – did you ever think of that? Maybe we're struggling against much vaster implications than those of our own bodies.'

He washed the windows; he dusted the furniture and blinds. Every weekend he stripped the bed, washed the sheets and slipcovers. He wasn't trying to accomplish deeds, but only to secure his position in a constellation of secret orbits and perilous hunches. He was trying to live his life alone in the house without Audrey.

Sometimes he managed to forget about her entirely. He sat on the sofa and read newspapers and magazines, or watched television. Sometimes his father or sister called, and he told them everything was OK. Audrey looked good. She seemed to enjoy her meal this afternoon. She seemed happy to see him. Sitting alone in the house, he felt the subdural vault of space rearing underneath the floorboards, the white skirling spaces out there beyond the roof, the hard enduring spaces inside his mouth and bony face. You move out into the indefinable limits of space all alone, he thought. And then, if you're lucky, you get to come back again. Maybe things between himself and Audrey weren't exactly what anyone would call ideal, but at least they were still talking. At least they were still making an effort.

'How are you feeling today, honey?'

'OK, I guess. I've got a little crick in my neck.'

'Would you like one of my famous back rubs?'

'Not right now. Maybe later.'

'Do you need anything from the house? Would you like me to bring any of your things?'

Harry visited her every day, but Audrey never needed anything.

Now he was alone in the house, looking around at the darkening spaces. Spaces between furniture, walls, windows, doors. Invisibly, imperceptibly, he was taking those spaces into his lungs, into the texture of his skin, into the intimate muscled architecture of his tongue and his heart. He knew it as well as he knew his own face. It was as simple as pain, as obvious as metal. Audrey was his wife. Audrey lived in his house and slept in his bed. Soon he would drive to the clinic and bring his wife Audrey back home again.

Beyond the Blue Mountains

PENELOPE LIVELY

Myra and George Purbeck, aboard the 'Empress of Sydney', rode through the Hawkesbury River valley. The 'Empress of Sydney' was a coach, of an extravagance that neither had ever before experienced, a double-decker with picture windows of tinted glass, luxuriantly upholstered seating and small tilted movie screens lest the voyager should weary of the landscape. From time to time a stewardess plied them with coffee or freshly squeezed orange juice. The air conditioning was just right; the restful and uninsistent background music was interrupted periodically by a voice which delivered a laconic, informative and sometimes witty account of the passing scene. They had been given a run-down of the social composition of suburban Sydney, with a digression on architectural style. They had learned about the crops grown in the farmland through which they now passed and about breeds of cattle and of sheep. 'Look left and you'll see three black swans on a billabong. The black swan is native to Australia.' Myra listened with interest.

She said, 'Is it the driver who does this commentary, do you imagine?'

'Presumably.' George was reading – intermittently – a copy of the London *Financial Times*. He was also, of course, gathering strength for the next leg of an exacting business trip. It was Sunday. The coach trip was for Myra's benefit: a kindly indulgence.

In Sydney, while George performed business, she had wandered at first jet-lagged and punch-drunk. She felt as though she had stepped into an alternative universe. The birds that flew in the garden of their hotel were little parrots, she saw with astonishment. The trees and shrubs were eerie and beautiful developments of familiar trees and shrubs. The very air seemed different. Then she had gone into an art gallery and seen on the walls a further miraculous transformation of the known world. The paintings showed a brilliant landscape, vibrant with colour – blues and golds and a bright ochre, a place of rock and dust and tree that was vast, bold and disturbing. Some of the pictures were of forest scenes – they depicted dappled light, sparkling water and exuberant growth. In one, an aborigine family camped around a fire in a clearing. Wallabies grazed, the trees were roped with flowering vines, shafts of light fell on emerald grass. Myra gazed in fascination; words she did not normally use flew into her head – a glade, an arcadian glade. Emerging once more into the heat and sunshine of the city, she was elated. The jet-lag faded. She began to feel unusually alert and well.

In the evenings they dined with business associates of George's, who asked her what she thought of Oz and then moved on to other matters without listening to her answer. George smiled benignly and sometimes he replied on her behalf, saying that Myra was having a fine old time in the shopping malls. He had brought her on this trip because she was on his conscience.

The coach began to climb. They had left the farmland behind and were entering the foothills of the Blue Mountains. The Blue Mountains, explained the invisible commentator, are thus named because of the sun's effect on the haze of oil vapour given off by eucalyptus trees. At the beginning of the nineteenth century they formed an impenetrable barrier between the expanding settlement and the hinterland beyond, until the pioneering expedition of Blaxland, Lawson and Wentworth in 1813 which led to the construction within six months of the first road through the mountains by hand-picked convict labourers.

Myra looked through the rose-tinted windows of the 'Empress of Sydney' at the steep slopes, the rock, the soaring trees. The coach now swung around hairpin bends.

She said, 'Six months . . . It's incredible.'

George was busy with his laptop. He lifted his eyes and stared for a few moments out of the window. He became reflective. Myra doubted that his thoughts were on Blaxland, Lawson and Wentworth or, indeed, the convicts.

The coach was sparsely populated. Up here on the top deck there were six immaculately suited Japanese who sat together in a cluster, a couple of backpacking American girls, and a waste of empty seats. The commentator began to talk of flora and fauna. He told the passengers to look for tree ferns, for casuarinas and for sulphur-crested cockatoos. When they reached the viewpoint and the revolving restaurant they must take a stroll and listen for bell-birds. If anyone had any questions feel free to hand a note to the stewardess.

Myra tore a page out of her diary. She wrote, 'What are the scarlet flowers on low bushes?' She gave it to the stewardess.

Five minutes later, the coach drew up at the roadside. Myra, looking down through the window, saw a lanky figure drop from the driver's compartment and vanish into the undergrowth of the steep hillside. A minute later he reappeared, leapt back up into the coach. They moved off once more. 'In fifteen minutes or so we shall reach the famous viewpoint, where you have a two-hour stop to enjoy the wonderful views beyond the Blue Mountains. Take a ride across the valley on the funicular railway, have a walk in the bush but be careful to stick to the paths – easy to get lost in this country. And you'll get a fine three-course meal in the revolving restaurant. Have a good time. And for the passenger who's interested in flowers – it's red honey-flower. Mountain Devil, we call it.'

The stewardess had arrived at Myra's elbow. She held out a tray on which was perched a spray of silky scarlet flowers. 'With the driver's compliments.'

Myra picked up the flowers. 'Thank you.' She tucked them into the top buttonhole of her shirt. She felt a surge of gaiety, a swoop of well-being which exactly matched the exuberance of the blossoms.

They arrived at their destination – a complex of cafés and restaurants at the highest point of the mountain range. The various viewpoints looked out across an apparently endless sequence of blue-green ridges splashed here and there with the rich brown of a rock-face. Myra, alighting from the coach, was again seized with exhilaration. This place is doing something to me, she thought. It was as though she had shed a skin, and stepped out new-minted and charged with life.

There were the restaurants, and the ticket office for the funicular railway which swooped dizzyingly down over the mountain-side. And there all around them beyond the car park were stretches of dappled woodland that made her think at once of that painting. She saw tree ferns, with grey scaly trunks and a brilliant eruption of bracken-like leaves. She saw the ropes of flowering creepers, the bright grass on which quivered gold coins of sunlight. She looked for grazing wallabies, and a tranquil aborigine family.

She said, 'Let's go for a walk.'

But George preferred to sit on the restaurant terrace with a beer. He had some phone calls to make, too. Ah yes, thought Myra, no doubt. 'Fine,' she said. 'I'll walk for a bit and come back for lunch. In this revolving restaurant, I suppose.'

She visited the toilets and then set off. She chose a narrow path which looked the least frequented, and followed it into the trees. And instantly she heard a bell-bird – a clear, sweet, chiming sound from some invisible presence high in the waving branches.

The trees thinned out. There was a clearing. And there in the clearing, leaned up against a rock reading a newspaper, with a sandwich in one hand and a can of coke alongside, was a man. A long, rangy man in ubiquitous Aussie gear – shirt, shorts and knee-socks. Myra prepared to walk tactfully past.

He looked up. 'Hi, there,' he said. 'Enjoying the trip?'

She put two and two together. Of course. The driver. 'I certainly am. And thank you for the flowers.'

'My pleasure.'

She had slowed up only very slightly. Now she was alongside him, and starting to move away.

'Take care,' he said. 'Stick to the path.'

'I will,' said Myra. 'And I heard a bell-bird.'

'Great,' said the driver. He was looking directly at her and the look, she suddenly saw, was one of appreciation, genial and in no way offensive. I like what I see, it said. Maybe we could have got together, under other circumstances.

He raised his paper. She walked on.

Well, thought Myra. Well.

She was not a vain woman, never had been. She saw herself, objectively, as the sort of person who is not much noticed. Unassertive. This, perhaps, accounted for much.

And now, here, in this interesting other world, she felt different. And, it would seem, appeared differently.

The path looped round in a circle and returned her to the car park and to the restaurant terrace. She cruised in, walking tall, hungry, brisk and seeing everything sharp and clear. Her husband, sitting there with his laptop, his newspaper and his beer.

They sat opposite one another in the revolving restaurant. Myra chose a seafood salad, avoiding the *filet* of buffalo with *confit* of beetroot. George ate a steak, medium rare.

They spoke, briefly, of arrangements for the following day, of a handbag Myra had purchased for her sister, of a difficulty George was experiencing with his computer. Myra told him of the bell-bird. She spoke of other birds she had noticed – the rosellas in the hotel garden, a kookaburra on a gatepost by the roadside. As she talked she saw the mountain ranges inch slowly past George's head. They sat within a creeping sphere, a dramatic and sumptuous backcloth quite at odds with the clatter of knives and forks, the red checked napery and the chomping diners. Myra's sense of disorientation became acute. Disorientation, and a certain wild confidence.

George was not listening to her. He was looking beyond her left shoulder. His eyes were blank. She knew what he was thinking about. He was thinking about Bridget Cashell, his mistress.

She said, 'You're thinking about Bridget Cashell, your mistress, aren't you?'

Mistress. She relished the word. It had overtones of satin dressing gowns. Bridget Cashell was in fact accounts manager in George's firm and although distinctly personable was not at all the satin dressing-gown type. Myra listened to her own words with astonishment and satisfaction.

George too listened, apparently. His eyes leapt to life. Myra saw surprise, dismay, and a process of rapid thought.

He said, at last, 'I didn't realise you knew, Myra.' He had rejected prevarication, it seemed.

'Oh, yes.'

She thought, and what's more, all of a sudden, out here, I know that I don't really love you any more. She watched him. He looked away. He pushed his plate aside, the food uneaten.

'Did you get her on the phone all right, just now?'

'It's the middle of the night, in England.'

'Of course – how silly of me. You could try this evening.'

'Please, Myra,' he said.

They sat in silence for a while. Myra finished her seafood salad, which was excellent. Many times, back home, in that other world where it was the middle of the night, she had thought about having this conversation but it had never, in the head, been at all like this.

'Myra . . . ' he began.

She picked up the menu. 'Do you want a dessert? I'm having tropical fruit salad. Papaya, guava . . . What's pawpaw, do you know?'

He shook his head. 'Myra, I'm finding it hard to know what to say . . .'

'Never mind,' she said, quite kindly. 'You've had a shock.'

She observed him. Behind his head, the Blue Mountains smoothly revolved. His face had a shrivelled look; he sat hunched into his chair. It occurred to Myra that he had become slightly smaller within the last few minutes. He was a big man normally, who sat erect.

Her next words rose quite unconsidered to her lips. 'Do you want to get rid of me and marry her?'

As soon as she had spoken she saw that she had hit the jackpot. George's eyes were eloquent with panic.

'No. No, Myra. Absolutely not. The last thing I . . . Look, should we talk about all this here? Wouldn't it be better if we sit down quietly back at the hotel . . . Or maybe when we get home to England, when we've both had a chance to think a bit.'

'I've been thinking,' said Myra. 'Quite a bit, really. But you may be right. We'll leave it, then. Sure you don't want any dessert?'

They finished the meal. Not in silence, for Myra chatted of the scenery and of their fellow eaters and George, wearing still this strange diminished look, responded wanly to her comments. He agreed that the Japanese were obsessed with photography. He turned to note the grove of casuarinas that she pointed out. On the walk back to the coach he listened – fruitlessly – for the bell-bird.

The driver stood by the door. He said to Myra, 'Hi, there,' and Myra smiled. The passengers resumed their seats, the coach started up and began the slow twisting descent down from the unfettered vistas of the mountain ranges and into the neat and structured universe of the Hawkesbury River valley and the wide road to Sydney. The commentary ceased. A movie came on; headphones were distributed.

George sat holding his newspaper, but did not turn the pages. And Myra saw now that they would not talk, either at the hotel or back home in England. What had passed between them would remain for ever beyond the Blue Mountains, potent and powerful. She felt a touch sorry for Bridget Cashell. And possibly for George.

✂ *Mea Culpa*

DAVID WIDGERY

'So. What am I supposed to do about it?' said Meyer for the third time that morning, his shoulders hunched with exasperation. 'The flat is too small, far too small. They all are. But I'm a doctor not a social worker. Go to the damned Housing Department about it.' The Bangladeshis before him looked dolefully at the grimy lino, defeated by the doctor's wrath. As the doctor had intended. Why does the whole bloody family have to come anyway? thought Meyer as he scrawled a prescription for paracetamol suspension to prove to himself he was indeed a doctor.

'Housing-man says, "You go to your doctor,"' protested the defeated Mr Miah as he fumbled with the consulting-room door-knob, which had worked loose with constant turning. Miah, whose last job had been in a Luton smelting works fourteen years ago, had married on a trip to Sylet and produced four Bethnal Green children with his sad young wife, Jana Bibi. He wore his hair comb-ploughed like a Denis Compton Brylcreem advert, no hat and an English jumble-sale suit. The combination made him look much older than his years. His children, in trainers and an odd mixture of bomber jackets and ankle-length skirts, were using Mrs Bibi's yellow sari alternately as a screen from the doctor and to wipe their snotty noses. 'You tell housing wallah, fuck off from Meyer,' the GP bellowed as they filed out. They departed to join another queue at the end of which someone else would say they had to go elsewhere. The doctor walked, shaking his head, to the sink to squirt his NHS aerosol, which restored the proper smell of institutional rectitude to the surgery. And balefully pressed the bell for the next customer.

By the end of the morning, he was exhausted. Twenty-two patients, seven referral letters, three complaining about waiting-list delays and admission cancellations, a row on the phone with a stuck-up paediatric registrar and a wrestling match to extract a stinking piece of Lego from a baby's ear hole. Some fool on the phone wanted him to send money to NHS SOS. Like every other day, alternating between the headlines of life: rape, violence and sudden death, and the small ads: worms, toothache and athlete's foot. Someone had even asked him for a new corset. A decent lass he had helped through depression, positive smear tests and a sad abortion was leaving London, because of 'the schools'. He saw a couple he had known since he started the practice forty years ago. The husband was growing steadily more demented after a bad stroke. Once alert and elegant, he was now sufficiently deranged to require constant nursing by his wife. She was now 'a carer', whether she liked it or not. And she did not. 'Carer', dreadful word. NHS SOS, indeed, might as well be CU, B and Q. He took the sherry bottle down from beside the urine-testing equipment and poured his first of the day.

He stared intently across the barbed wire and security-barred window to the railway line and the flats beyond. He could remember before there were council flats. When the close was a little world of its own, where everyone minded everybody else's business but no one went much further than Liverpool Street, except in case of war. In those days he had presided over birth and death in people's front rooms. Doctors were respected then, even truculent Jewish ones like Meyer. 'The more people say against you, the more I agree with you,' a patient had told him in his first year as a GP, which he had spent overturning the medical mismanagement of his predecessor. Didn't do midder now, the hospitals had taken that over years ago. People went off to the Hospice to die. And he hadn't used his sink-side microscope for decades. His medical-instrument cupboard was also covered with a thick layer of dust, a museum of previous enthusiasms. When he had enthusiasm. He'd won a medal for child health but nowadays didn't do much with the kids except give them paracetamol for their endless influenza. Meyer was fed up. Meyer, Miah, what's the difference? We come here from God knows where and try and make the best of things. Our children hate us for it and then we die. Mea culpa. 'The only wisdom I have ever learnt in this job', he used to say, 'is that the good die young . . . and in considerable pain.' He could still smell the cheap fat smell of London when he, Whitechapel-born, walked with new Jewish arrivals in flight from Vienna and Berlin and tried to persuade them that the museums and parks made up for the awfulness of what passed for café life: Lyons, ABC and the Express Dairies. Reflectively he sprayed some more aerosol.

'God wasn't a social worker,' he also used to say, often to social workers. In fact Harry was sure he was harsh, cruel and terrifying. That's why people worshipped him. But he had imagined God as some sort of heavenly social-democrat. Now he didn't any more. The Spanish Civil War, the defence of Stalingrad, the Sputnik, had once been Meyer's litany. Then things had become more modest; the NHS, the BBC and comprehensive schools. But now Doctor Harry, kosher product of the Communist culture of Whitechapel, wasn't so sure any more. He sat on the surgery table scowling at the *Telegraph* which he nowadays read (for the sport). It had an editorial entitled 'Socalism RIP'. It was easy to say now that we were naïve about Russia, but people don't understand what it was like then. A bit befuddled a couple of nights ago he'd read aloud the titles of the Left Book Club editions which stood in a demoralised line in his large draughty library. They didn't make a word of sense and he tried to reassure himself with familiar passages. S. Leff on public health, old Sam, whatever became of him? *The Post-War History of the British Working Class* by Allen Hutt. Stuart Gelder on the Chinese Communists. What about Tienanmen Square? Orwellian stuff. But then he's never approved of Orwell and still wouldn't have the stuff in the house. 'Are you still up, Harry?' his wife shouted from the kitchen, where she chainsmoked with *Art and Artists*. 'For God's sake, I'm off to bed.' They'd met at a Left Zionist talk at the Whitechapel Gallery nearly fifty years ago, against Mosley in their teens, for a Second Front as young doctors. Miriam had been a consultant pathologist by the time of the Committee of 100 so she signed the letter to *The Times* and it was Harry who got arrested in Trafalgar Square.

Why exactly does Miriam smoke so much nowadays? he brooded over more sherry. She'd taken it up with characteristic bloody-mindedness when the final damning Medical Research Council trials were published. 'When the London air is clean, then I shall give up my pleasures,' she'd decreed. 'Harry,' she shouted round the library door, 'you do too much for other people.' Meyer knew that. He didn't need his wife to echo it and then retreat. He didn't need his children to dread him for his temper. He needed them, as they used to be, young and dependent and admiring. So that he had tangible reasons to soldier on through the slums of East London all the hours God gave him. It was the kids more than Miriam he came home to when eventually he got back home. It was their enquiring optimism which always prevented him from losing faith. But he didn't see much of either of them now and Miriam and he hardly talked except to grumble. He could no longer rely on them to protect him from doubt. And doubt it certainly was. Since 1956, the invasion of Budapest, he'd adopted a public scepticism about politics. But he, and everyone else, knew where he stood. Somehow this camouflage of irony had, by a process of political osmosis, become absorbed into his real identity. Over the last three years, with the apparent disintegration of the Soviet Union, he was no longer so sure it was a disguise. He was afraid he'd become a cynic.

It wasn't just politics. There had been a time when he'd been as devoted to medicine as to a lover, stayed up late with the journals, interrogated visiting consultants and measured haemoglobin in the surgery sink. In fact what had drawn him into the CP was as much its zeal for science as the fight against fascism. The Party in those days had a good wad of scientists, historians and poets. People you could admire. Nowadays who was there? He only read the *British Medical Journal* for the obituaries.

Always argumentative, he often thought 'the line' as imparted by callow youths from King Street whose acne he'd often treated himself was batty. In fact he'd probably have been thrown out long before he left in 1956 if they didn't need his monthly sub. But medicine in the slums of the East End managed to make sense of what the zealots mangled. There were the masses all right, huddled but individuals, rich in their own lousy contradictions. If only they could get organised, they would begin to function not as separate atoms but more like the great interacting cycles of cellular biochemistry. Meyer had always loved molecular biology and once heard the great Hans Krebs lecturing on the cascades of enzymes which made the cell productive. To him politics and medicine had to be about biology and he was suspicious when he heard either called a science. He had a tendency to ignore the ugly pieces of political certainty which were handed down from the branch committee and the *Daily Worker* editorials. It was the sombre thrill of death, the vernal delight of birth, the low comedy of the sickbed which made some sense out of the messiness of humanity. Not that he was a liberal. Or like the other doctors whose idea of culture was Chekhov at the National Theatre, and whose philosophy was what passed for philosophy in nineteenth-century provincial Russia, people saying, 'What's the point of it all?' They do it to this day, he groaned, in their wretched Postgraduate Centre. And Christians! Makes me long for Bertie Russell and that bunch of Stalinists at King Street. What ever else was wrong with them, they weren't self-pitying.

Meyer's proletariat wasn't a historical instrument but something that cried and shouted and made love. Sometimes shouted back at him. But he forgave it for caring more about its pain than his dignity. So he believed. He believed the thanks of repeatedly reassured Cockney mothers, allowed himself to be slyly flattered by the intoxicated Irishmen who said he'd surely go to Heaven, and easily accepted with token protests the deference of the ingratiates for whom he backdated sick notes. And beneath the irony he donned as habitually as his brown army-style anorak, he believed there was a point to his work. And that the work fell into a larger march of human progress. When he arrived in his patients' sick rooms he seemed to fill them with conviction. His businesslike manner and easy familiarity made the patients feel safer. His medical equipment was held, not in the conventional doctor's Gladstone, but in a small shopping bag as if to announce that he didn't need any artifice. But everything was exactly what he wanted and where he needed it. He was Dr Meyer and that was enough.

The phone rang. It was the secretary of the consultant psychiatrist apologising that he couldn't do a domicilliary for at least two days because he was at a conference on Inner City Health Care in Ottowa. 'That's marvellous,' he snapped. 'I'll tell my patient to stop dementing for another couple of days.' He remembered when he used to do home visits with Len Cohen, who set up the cardiology department at the London (he was damned if he was going to call it the bloody Royal London Trust). Len was a fairly competent general physician and a good raconteur who called himself a cardiologist because he had got hold of an ECG machine early on and loved to play about with it in people's bedrooms. Meyer used to mock him gently out of hearing of the patient about his squiggly bits of electrocardiogram paper. 'So what are you going to do if he's had an antero-lateral infarct, Len? Just the same as I'm doing in any case. Bed rest.' Len had died only last year of a heart attack like so many doctors. He'd had a grainy old photograph in the *BMJ* obituaries which had talked of his war service, love of bridge and devoted surviving wife in the manner of *BMJ* obituaries. Didn't mention he'd been the secretary of the Communist Party's London medical section in the early 1950s and fixed up all the vital divisional votes when it looked as if the British Medical

Association might succeed in sabotaging the foundation of the NHS. Those were the days, before the Cold War set in, when we had dreams and were young enough to do something about them. Meyer still remembered the East End he came back to from the Services, knocked to pieces with wreckage strewn from here to Essex, the docks rubble, most of the people gone, many of them dead. But there was optimism then, Russia wasn't a dirty word and socialism, that was something noble, clean and unquestionable.

It was one thirty and he was due for lunch. He'd reluctantly arranged to meet a school friend in the Aphrodite Steak House. Well, buy him lunch that amounted to. It was Ben Hagan, who lived in Greatorex Street and had been a bit of a ladies' man when Meyer had got his head stuck in the anatomy textbooks. He'd wound up as a full-time trade union organiser for the Lady Garment Workers' Union and often sent Meyer invites for political meetings. Meyer had been once to the Conway Hall when Ben was on the platform, mid-1950s, during the Suez crisis. With a Labour MP who Meyer knew ran a big import-export racket in and out of Eastern Europe, a Cypriot Communist with red hair, who spouted a lot that you couldn't understand, and Ben, who still looked handsome but hadn't ever settled down. Ben was not a good speaker Meyer thought, too quiet and no jokes, still going on about the 'International Movement' and what Labour would or wouldn't or should or shouldn't do. He remembered Ben at the huge anti-Suez demo when Bevan spoke and ball bearings were rolled under the mounted police. 'The tanks, they've sent tanks into Budapest,' the Party members were whispering to each other in the mêlée. Disbelieving.

The Aphrodite Steak House was an odd place which Meyer only got to know when one of the waiters became manic depressive and filled the Aphrodite's sinks with heaps of potatoes and unwashed plates. Stupid social worker with a silly swirling dress and nipples you could hang your hat on kept asking him how he knew the patient was mad when he, Meyer, couldn't speak Turkish? Then the waiter tried to put her in the sink too. It was a typical East End steakhouse, bank managers and business lunches at dinner time, minor criminals and closing-time drunks in the evening. Bloody big steaks with Black Forest gâteau and house white which tasted of aftershave.

Ben was hovering outside, looking a lot older as they slapped each other's backs and finessed the ritual. It turned out that Ben was still in the digs in Lewisham to which he moved to be near the union headquarters. He'd spent years living out of suitcases, haggling votes in conference-hall bars and being snarled at by strikers. All for a union watch and a TUC long-service medal. 'Harry, the only bloke who could memorise the whole of the *Daily Worker* editorial verbatim and then deliver it just as if he had thought it up himself on the spur of the moment.' 'Ben, whatever happened to that Irish lass on the district committee you used to take out for advanced theoretical training?'

'Well, you should laugh, Meyer,' said Ben when they had exchanged pleasantries about manic waiters with the manager and ordered their prawn cocktails and steaks. 'I was at a Party history meeting last weekend, well we don't call it the Party any more. About the British Party, as it was then, and the Russians. Anyway there was George Mathews who, God knows, hasn't got long. And on the same platform Peter Fryer, you remember the *Worker*'s correspondent in Budapest in 1956, whose reports they wouldn't publish. And what does old George say? "I'm sorry Peter. I was wrong. We should have published them. I'm sorry." Talk about mea culpa. Fryer just smiles. But you know old Sadie Connor, the lawyer's mother? She proceeds to have a heart attack and the whole proceedings came to a standstill while we wait for an ambulance. Which, as you know, what with Thatcherism, takes ages. Still, it being a Party meeting, that is – I'd better start to get this right – a Democratic Movement meeting, there were plenty of doctors.' I hope they brought their damn ECGs, thought Meyer as he poured the aftershave. What the hell does it matter who apologises to whom, we don't believe in heaven do we, for God's sake? As ever, there was something about Hagan he couldn't help admiring.

'So you, Ben, how goes it? How is the Party or the Democratic Movement or whatever it is?' They were on to the Black Forest gâteau and a second carafe of wine now. 'Me?' said Ben. 'Me, I'm expelled that's what.' He went on to say that the new democratic opposition who took over the Party from the hard liners proceeded to expel more people than ever before. 'Loyalty oaths, Harry! I was required to sign a pledge that I would not engage in "factionalism". Me who joined in '34 at the age of twelve.'

Well, you look older than seventy, Ben, in fact you look to me very like wheelchair material pretty soon and then who's going to look after you? No more delegations to the Black Sea by the sound of it, thought Harry beneath his listening smile.

'I got a very nice send off from the Union, you know. And the old gang still meet. Remember Sam and Mollie, who retired to Eastbourne? He's still a stalwart of the Labour Party and publishes books on East London history. They turned up for the presentation.'

As they parted Ben, too wizened to be still handsome, Meyer impatient to make a home visit before afternoon surgery started, Meyer felt a sort of tightening in his chest which he dismissed as a sentimental pang. He gave Hagan a farewell embrace, clutching him harder than he intended, then recoiling somewhat embarrassed. And as he drove the old Rover towards Rothschild Buildings he remembered an elderly Croatian florist at Number 32 with breast cancer he'd looked after. Then another Balkan tragedy, Dubrovnik under bombardment, glowing as boats burnt in the harbour like a Verdi opera. He remembered the holiday he took there with Miriam. In fact he'd preferred Yugoslavia to Israel, not so many maniacs about. But the waiter had spilt his chips every single night. 'At my age,' he'd told Miriam, 'you don't go on holiday any more to have your chips spilt.' In front of a zebra crossing in Bethnal Green Road he slowed the car, thinking of the road to Basra, seeing some anonymous bugger burnt alive at the wheel of his jeep just trying to get out of the bloody mess. Six hundred and forty oil rigs ablaze and the sky black and the roads smothered with brown dust. Sirens in Tel Aviv and Haifa and his sister-in-law learning how to put on a gas mask again. Meyer remembered the Warsaw Ghetto museum near Haifa which he'd been to once on a CND doctors' exchange, where he'd seen photo-enlargements of the leaflets issued by the heroic, betrayed Jewish resistance.

Then, apparently peering over the top of a tank-sized skip, Boris Yeltsin's suspiciously corpulent face alight with ire. Yeltsin, on top of a Soviet tank outside the Moscow White House after Gennady Yanayev and his vodka-sodden putchists. And the ozone layer! What a triumph of science and manufacturing to make our entire planet at last uninhabitable. It's impossible to understand any more. And I don't know why I should. I used to want to be a good doctor, now I just hope I don't end up in a malpractice suit.

Turning his Rover into Bethnal Green Road he drove past the old hospital now closed and boarded up. Its entrance was still elegant with porticoes and rococo window frames. There was a large yellow hoarding offering it For Sale mounted in the front garden where the porters used to plant daffodils and tulips. Next to it was a ruined tennis court on which the doctors and nurses used to knock up in the hot summers while patients in their pyjamas watched. Beside the hospital was a council building which had been a stronghold of the Party in the days of Red Stepney and which Meyer had often visited for meetings and for patients as a young doctor, when it was an unruly place of noise, bustle and children. Now it was converted by the council into private 'executive housing' but remained unlet, executives desirous of an address in the Cambridge Heath Road having proved rather scarce. The closed-down hospital made him angry but the unlet apartments cheered him up. And for a moment made him feel a lot happier. There was, he allowed himself to reflect, something rather marvellous among the Bangladeshis, their sheer youth and fertility and fecundity and the way the children had to weave and bob through customs and cultures. He would write another letter about the Miahs. Traffic was awful, it seemed always to be getting worse. Meyer sat watching two bricklayers clad in tee-shirts and trainers filling in the front of what had been a large clothing factory. Allwear Fashions. In one of the deserted factory windows someone had carefully stencilled 'Arsenal: The Greatest' so that it could be read from the road.

Perhaps that's what everything now felt to him, final. The mocking graffiti, the young alcoholic men already drunk on an arid patch of green opposite the surgery when he arrived at eight thirty this morning, the patients who despaired of ever finding work. Far from being swept along on the great free market, the East End was sinking in it. Even the pubs were boarded up, which had never happened in the 1930s. In fact, in some ways things were worse than he could ever remember them. Was this what he worked for in the street-corner soap-box sessions and the early days of the NHS and CND? As if to answer him, a large swastika appeared painted on the decrepit map outside Bethnal Green Gardens with the simple wording 'We're back.' Ridiculous and yet not ridiculous. These reactions were all over Europe. France, Schleswig-Holstein, Baden-Wurttenburg. The Dutch, the Swiss and the Italians. And us. The ruins of the East European economies are confronted not by a triumphant West but by a global system which is itself stagnant. If human society fails to progress, it falls back, he remembered Ben saying. One of Ben's truer truisms.

I may be confused about Yugoslavia but I'm certain about one thing, he said to himself self-reprovingly. Societies, well societies like the East End, don't stay put. They are fought over, their values are challenged, their cultures the subject of argument all the time. And now something is happening which is more important than the misspelt graffiti and the boarded-up hospitals, the silly architecture and the pot-holed roads. There is a new philosophy about which says no one is responsible for what is happening, that the mess is just a kind of accident. And we, who should know better, are being told to keep quiet about it. Cultivate our damned gardens. Well, whatever else he was, Meyer grunted to himself, he wasn't going to be one of those East European turncoats who changed their ideology as often as was necessary to keep hold of their privileges. Maybe to keep his beliefs he would have to disbelieve his faith. He remembered a Polish Catholic priest he'd met in Prague who'd been imprisoned by the régime for nearly fifteen years and kept his faith alive by constant prayer, reading and reflection. Then, when he got out and the Church became legal and he started to draft his first sermon, he realised that he didn't believe in God any longer. So instead he pleaded with his rough peasant listeners not to drink so much vodka and told the men not to beat their wives and children. Meyer understood that now. It's the people who give the faith, not the other way round.

It was up to him, of all people, not to betray his faith. Because his beliefs, or the best of them, were not abstractions but shaped by his work with his patients. Ill people, ill-housed and ill-fed and ill-used people. There was something he could still feel, under all his exhaustion and bitterness and loneliness, a sort of force which he had witnessed in birth and death, in grief and elation, in the sardonic wit of everyday life. Something he needed to be in contact with more than he liked to admit.

The bloody NHS which he battled with and cursed every day of his working life, now that was something that mattered, a different set of values, an Atlantis of values and experience. Meyer was tired and he was bitter too, but he had made a kind of decision. He would turn up at the Postgraduate Centre that evening for the first time in years and even if he didn't know any of the young doctors, he would insist on talking about Mile End Hospital and the wards they were proposing to close down.

It was then that the pain hit him, a wrenching blow to his chest causing him to groan out loud, a numbing extension down his left arm which made it difficult to hold the car's steering wheel and each intake of breath a gasped ordeal. The London Chest Hospital was up ahead and he tried to steer the Rover on towards it. But with terrible difficulty.

Meyer's funeral was in Edmonton at the Orthodox Jewish Burial Ground. Somehow orthodoxy had taken him over. Women and men were separate, there were many official mourners who had not known him and few who did. Miriam stood alone in a state of shock. The Chair of the Postgraduate Centre had found her way there and stood with a white paper skull cap to show respect. The funeral cart took him through the grim grey stones and men with hats and beards lowered his coffin. Other men queued to place handfuls of earth over it. Ben Hagan stood at the back expecting someone to say something about Meyer's part in the NHS and support for progressive causes, but the priest only mentioned his medical work.

The Expulsion

MARSHA ROWE

The space that surrounded her did not contain her. Her consciousness lay in part outside her. She was not herself aware that she did not fully occupy the space in which she moved. To the world around her, objects, other people, she attributed many of the feelings that originated in her. It was a classic case of projection. The lack of clear boundaries, being unacknowledged, was like fear. She lived in fear that emptiness would engulf her. Since she did not fully occupy the world, she could not fully enjoy its pleasures. She lived a half life.

When she had a baby, the baby shared in that half life.

A rope of sound alerted Miranda, and a precise Asian voice from the loudspeaker, 'Ladies and gentlemen, we realise the alarm is sounding in the airport. If it is discontinuous you may remain where you are. If it is constant please vacate the area immediately.' Was it a bomb? Miranda stood up. When she saw that no one else was leaving she sat down again with a strange, vacant feeling that she thought was the absence of panic. She looked up at the destination board. Her flight was delayed thirty minutes. She decided to take a walk, picked up her bag and went towards the Ladies.

Once there she stood in front of the mirror and hitched up her secondhand 501s. They were weird, she judged. Indigo was the only dye that adhered to the outside of the thread and faded like this to reveal a sort of pattern of the body's shape, like another's imprint. She took her Mason Pearson from her bag and brushed her coarse fair hair out into an electrified nimbus. She decided not to buy secondhand jeans again. The baggy legs looked at odds with her own. What if she explored that idea in one of her textile designs? Could a personal story be suggested through the properties of a cloth?

Flight AZ 1261 boarding Gate Seven. That was her flight. Her nerves turned to freeways. She put the hairbrush back in her bag.

She had checked in late and been allocated the last available seat, at the back, in smoking. She sat down and switched the air-conditioning nozzle on full to blow straight down over her and clear the air. It made her feel cold. She asked the steward for a rug, spread it over her knees, and adjusted her watch to an hour ahead.

At one thirty Italian time the plane dived through clouds to a smooth touchdown at Pisa Airport, although the flight had been rumbly and the engine noisy as an old banger, Miranda thought.

In the passport queue two Indian women were ushered aside to have their papers examined and an Irishman in front of her watched nervously while the pages of some Euro document of his were turned and turned again. Finally, his document stamped, the Irishman smiled in relief and moved on. Miranda slid her passport under the glass with its new photo of her and Toby together, Toby looking startled, as he had been at the time, by the flash of the camera. She wondered stupidly whether the officer would ask where her baby was, and then, thinking what nonsense, it's none of his business, watched him flick through her passport, glance at her, stamp it.

Her Moroccan bag was easy to spot on the carousel. She heaved it on to her shoulder, and then there was Louis on the edge of a small crowd of eager faces, with his absent-minded look and his bright blond hair.

'Hi,' she said, grinning.

'Here, let me take this.' Louis took her bag and they walked away from the crowd. Louis put the bag down, took off his glasses and kissed her, folding his hand round the back of her neck in a way she disliked.

'How are you?' She pulled away, and then put her arms out again to embrace him, and felt his young torso firm in her clasp. He smelled differently. Of course he would after four weeks in Italy. Hadn't there been a softer feeling about him before? 'I was beginning to wonder if I'd ever see you again,' she said, letting go.

'It's been far too long,' he said. 'Let's sit down.'

'No, I've had enough of airports.'

'Wait here then. I'll buy your ticket. We have to take the train to Florence.'

A few puddles lay on the path between the airport terminal and the station. The air, fresh from rain, smelled of vanilla and aniseed. Beside the railway fence at the back of the platform was a box hedge studded by a series of taller bushes pruned into spheres. Miranda was reminded forcibly that this was Europe, this shaping of garden into ornament. The continent had assaulted her senses when she first arrived from Australia in her early twenties, its differences pressing against her as she had

stared and stared, more bewildered than she had expected to be
by the ancient scabby buildings, by high wooden doors behind
which secret lives were breathed, beyond her grasp,
unfathomable.

She had been hungry for it, for travel, for knowing it all. How
had she ended up now with Mick, in London, with a baby? She
climbed into the waiting train and sat admiring Louis as he
stretched upwards in his black leather jacket to push her bag on
to the rack. She congratulated herself on her good luck. Louis
was her passport to freedom, and back to herself.

'Six thousand five hundred lire for a single ticket,' Louis said,
sitting next to her.

'About three pounds?'

'That's right. For a journey that takes an hour. I tell you, the
Italian railway system is so much more efficient.' He kissed her
again. Miranda found it was not so easy to kiss him back.

She felt nothing for him, nothing at all. She pulled away,
flapped her hand around, and said, 'Touch wood. When I go
back we'll get a change of government. The polls put Labour two
points ahead this morning.' She smiled in amusement, 'Rosalind's
niece said that Major was broccoli-flavoured fizzy water. The
worst analogy an eleven-year-old could come up with.'

Louis sighed, 'Hey, it's so good to see you.'

'There's an election here too, I read. On Sunday.'

'From what I gather,' Louis nodded and said drily, taking her
hand again, 'you were more or less right when you wrote about
the corruption. You can't get any sort of a job, at least not in a
civic institution, without having the politics to match. Christian
Democrat, the PDs, or whatever.'

Miranda shrugged and looked out of the window. She watched
a man on a scooter herding a line of baggage trolleys along the

platform. A few late passengers hurried for the train. Gazing out at the clay-coloured apartment buildings she thought for some reason of that morning, months back, when she woke at eight and Toby, who had been fed at six, did not wake, and suddenly she was dressed and walking down the street towards the row of shops leaving Toby on his own in the house as if he did not exist, as if she had returned to the time before Toby, before she became, as it were, two people. She'd bought a newspaper and a croissant from the bakery, and wished for something else, some wicked and forbidden treat, then suddenly rushed back to the house remembering that she'd left Toby alone, abandoned him almost.

Whereas when she left Toby properly for the first time it had been in the care of Mick for a weekend, when Toby was to be weaned. Mick was quite capable of taking over for a couple of days and insisted that she should go away. She'd had no doubt that he was right and left feeling no grief. On the contrary. She'd been longing for independence. Just as, during her pregnancy, she longed to be slim and able to wear jeans again. One evening in particular she felt consumed by envy as she watched her friend Rosalind striding about looking capable and free in jeans while her own belly stretched and bulged and mysteriously she put on weight all over.

To be herself again, she thought, not tied any longer to the last evening feed.

Before she left that weekend she made sure that all the bedtime rituals were in place, ready to displace the feed itself. Toby tapped the bird mobile and watched it swing, said good night to the alphabet animals over the fireplace, happily lay back in his cot, while she sang 'Rock a Bye Baby'. She found she could never sing the line about letting the baby fall cradle and all. She replaced that line with something else, something that rhymed. Already she'd forgotten what other words she'd used.

So she spent the weekend away visiting an ex-student of Rosalind's – Louis – who'd moved to Otley. The three of them sat in Louis's tiny stone house drinking, talking, Rosalind curled up in an armchair, Miranda next to Louis on the couch. The extra weight Miranda gained during pregnancy was still with her then, although her belly was back to normal, with no stretch marks. Her breasts stung, expecting Toby to feed.

Her bare feet rested, at one point, against Louis. A buzz starting at her toes had winged up her legs, landing like a butterfly between them, where it stayed, persistent, until she changed position and put her legs firmly on the floor. When Louis touched her on the arm as they said good night desire looped up again, and later, lying in the strange bed in the strange house, she felt like a sleepwalker when she found herself leaving the room, walking out into the hall towards that touch, for more of it.

The train stopped at Pisa Centrale. Passengers crowded into their carriage. A group of lively young women bundled on to the seats opposite. The train set off again. Miranda looked back at Louis. She smiled and said hello as if she'd just arrived and sank back against the seat.

Across the aisle the most animated of the young women ran her hand through her long hair, pushing it off her brow in a youthful, assertive way, and glanced at Louis.

Jealousy grabbed Miranda. She sat stiffly, fighting irrationality, feeling marooned by its damp and cold. The train started to follow a river. She saw plastic left by floodwater caught in the bare winter branches, masses of greyish, labelless opaque stuff, an encampment of travellers on the opposite bank, allotments squeezed between the river and the railway track and then the landscape opened out into fields of gnarled vines, the occasional bloom of an almond tree in blossom and the dark line of cypresses against the afternoon sky. Did she have nothing to say to Louis? She turned and his eyes were as calm as the sea, and she relaxed. It was all right, she told herself. A month apart was a long time when they hardly knew each other. She felt the warmth of returning desire. The river reappeared. 'All that plastic hanging in the trees. Like the ghosts of birds,' she said.

'The Italians keep their houses spotless,' said Louis, 'but outside they don't care what rubbish they leave around.'

The taxi from the station took ten minutes, swerving past trolley buses and snarling mopeds. Women swung along the pavement in short flared coats with sandwich-board shoulders, scarves and hair clips all tucked and fastened, while the men seemed to stroll.

Outside the hotel, a brass name plate. Inside two guards in a bright cubbyhole under the stairs who registered their arrival then ignored them. 'That stairway leads up to a palace,' Louis nodded at a flight that vanished into drabness, 'which no one seems to enter and no one seems to leave.' The hotel was on the top floor. They took the lift. It was tiny and badly lit with a scuffed carpet and a yellowish mirror in which Miranda caught a sudden shocking image of herself – patchy skin, gaunt cheeks, hair wispy – while Louis stared without seeing either of them. Then Miranda saw him blink and he said, 'We're here.'

At the hotel desk a balding young man took their passports, picked out a blue tasselled key from the rack. They followed him along a hall hung with faded Renaissance prints, past a lounge, a roof garden at the turn of the stairs to a high, dark door at the end of a corridor.

The room was large. Miranda noticed a giant, scuffed blue wardrobe and matching chest of drawers with a rose marble top that took up the wall opposite the twin beds. She went to a footstool under the window and stepped up on it. She turned the latch, opened the window above and pushed back the shutters, letting in the steady grey light of the afternoon and the noise of the city. Looking back she saw Louis, his eyes oddly expressionless. He was waiting for her to make a move but, as at the airport, she felt nothing.

She looked out at the jumble of deserted balconies opposite, at the projecting eaves beneath the window which concealed the road below, and caught the fresh scent left by rain. She turned again and smiled at Louis, who came over and stood beside her. She took off his glasses and held his head in her hands.

They lay on the bed and lovemaking came more easily than it had done even during Louis's visits to London or her one visit to him. It was like that first night in Otley, when she'd crept into Louis's room and he'd sat up, dazed, then welcoming, after which she'd broken the news to Mick that she'd made love to someone else, someone younger, someone she met when she went away with Rosalind, whose name was Louis. Mick could now be free of her, if he wanted. At the time she sounded calm, and talked with nothing of the anger of their early rows during her pregnancy, when Mick moaned and held his head in his hands, saying he just wasn't prepared for a child, for that sort of commitment.

They slept. Louis woke to late afternoon. 'Get dressed quickly,' he whispered in her ear. 'I want to take you to San Lorenzo.'

Cars, scooters, Florentines, other tourists, narrow streets, a piazza. 'That is the Baptistery,' Louis said, looking over at an

octagon of green and white marble that was fuzzied, Miranda
thought, like something that had been under water for a very
long time. 'And that is the Duomo.' She raised her eyes to admire
the dome but already Louis was tugging at her arm, leading her
away down a narrow street, across another piazza and up some
wide shallow steps to the church. He pushed open the heavy
double doors and as they entered and walked down the nave
Miranda caught her breath at the vast cold space and the echoing
hush of visitors' voices. At the crossing he turned left down a
transept and took her through into a room panelled on two sides
and bordered by a running bench. 'This is the sacristy', he said
turning round, 'built by Brunelleschi for the Medici tombs.' He
glanced at her, his gaze insistent. Miranda walked over to the
central tomb and laid her hand on the circular bronze inlay on
the marble while Louis went on turning and explaining. 'Those
draped figures are by Donatello,' he pointed up at the cameos
pinning the ceiling corners. 'And the bronze shields with balls are
the sign of the Medici. No one knows what the balls were,
exactly. Coins, perhaps.'

'Dye?' she suggested. 'Dyers hung a blue ball outside their
premises.' She was determined to engage, to say something. She
thought of the pleasure of his smooth, hairless young chest, and
of his soft, pale skin.

'Perhaps,' he gave her one of his academic looks, attentive and
tolerant. 'Textiles were an enormously important trade in
Florence.'

Her attempt to sound interested fizzled out in uncertainty.
'I'm wrong,' she said. 'Dyers had no status, even though they
were organised here in Florence earlier than anywhere else.'
Louis looked at her dubiously and Miranda wondered, seeing his
glance shift away, whether she knew this young man at all. His

body was one thing. His work another. She knew so little about him.

'In the thirteenth century they had a religious brotherhood, with a hospital, just as if they were a guild,' she added, remembering with an effort her textile history, 'and then they did have a guild of their own, briefly, in the fourteenth century, which was suppressed. Probably with the help of your Medici.'

'Maybe,' Louis said, 'when they were establishing independence from the popes,' and went on with his lecture about the history of Florence, speaking gravely, turning away occasionally, thinking aloud. Listening to him, Miranda understood how absorbed Louis was by his research. Making love had been so easy, her happiness had seemed assured, at least for the weekend. But now she felt cramped by the cold of the place, or by its age that was suddenly too cavelike, all this grey stone and marble, and she pulled the scarf she'd worn higher up round her neck, and looked away. 'Let's go and see those bronze pulpits,' she said.

Louis showed her the rest of the church, then took her out into the cloister. Dusty oranges hung in the folded dark of a tree in the centre from which little paths radiated out to a collar of twiggy azaleas and mossy urns. Louis did not seem to notice. Instead he walked her round the arches and pointed across the cloister at the first floor. 'That', Louis whispered, his voice low with awe and historic weight, 'was the library designed by Michelangelo.' Miranda nodded.

'I'm tired,' she said.

'Let's go back to the piazza,' Louis said. 'I know where we can have an expensive coffee, somewhere you pay for the privilege of sitting down.'

At the café she again admired the Duomo, ate *petits fours*, listened to Louis tell her about his art restoration research, how much fun he had booking the hotel for her visit, how he loved her and missed her, how he'd hired a car to take her to Lucca, how he decided not to try to show her everything, but to select some special places.

They returned to the hotel. They planned to eat out later. Back in their room Miranda was drawn to the window. She stepped up on to the footstool and gazed out at the immersed glow of the terracotta. There was a darkened coin resting on a tile and moss on a lower roof. She turned to find Louis close, his face almost level as he stood beside her. Outside she was aware of the cool, damp air. Inside the room was warm and Louis' skin felt light and dry to her lips.

They undressed and lay side by side on the clean white sheets. Miranda felt clear of hesitation and doubt. Louis rested his hand on her belly and he too seemed content. The light pressure of his hand concentrated her attention. Slowly all her feelings gathered towards that place under his palm until, horrified, as if flung from safety, she found herself racked by sobs. After some minutes she heard herself say 'I miss Toby.'

At breakfast the waiter led them to a table on which a poinsettia stood with its flowers gone and its leaves turned yellow. Her mood this morning was calmer. Miranda said nothing about the night before. A woman guest sat reading. A frail old man made his way to a wallside table, where he was joined by another with a shining pink scalp. Miranda and Louis ordered coffee. The waiter served the old men cereal and fruit. Miranda dipped a croissant into her coffee, grateful for Louis's tactful silence. She watched the waiter return to his post by the coffee machine, where he opened a carton of orange juice to fill a half-empty jug and rearrange the yogurts. His tight-fitting blue jacket and gold epaulettes did nothing for his restless, disreputable air.

After breakfast Miranda rang London. Mick said hello and then put Toby on the phone and she heard his gurgle, but that was all. Did Toby recognise her voice?

They went out and walked across the Ponte Vecchio. The Arno was running fast and high, its water dun coloured. 'We really should have come here first,' said Louis as they entered the courtyard of Santa Maria del Carmine, 'but it doesn't open that early.' A row of cypresses swayed under the rain which just then pelted down in heavy drops. English schoolgirls stood under the arches. Miranda read a notice: Thirty visitors only allowed in at one time, for a period of fifteen minutes. Louis bought tickets. The attendant opened the gate, led them into a passageway, then out into the church. They turned again, and there was the Brancacci Chapel cordoned off by red rope.

At a glance Miranda took in high walls ringed by brightness, a swathe of reds, pinks, some sort of blue, above the bunched crowd of visitors. Light from a concealed source entered through a false central window above an altar that glowed with a gold Madonna. Miranda looked at Louis, who was watching her hesitantly as if he was no longer sure who she was or what she was doing there. She found a place between some onlookers on the far side from where she could see the frescoes. Louis joined her, brushed a hand back over his crew cut, a signal that he was about to explain his research. She said, 'Tell me what I'm seeing,' and made her voice warm and inviting.

'The first panel is Masaccio's "Expulsion",' Louis said. 'Yes,' said Miranda. She looked away towards its companion fresco on the facing wall, at an image of Adam and Eve still in paradise.

'That's not Masaccio,' Louis said. 'No,' said Miranda, observing the decorative prettiness of the mythical female-headed serpent staring at the stupefied figures. She turned back to face the 'Expulsion'. She moved away from Louis and mingled amongst the onlookers listening to their Italian guide. She looked up at the painting of the two banished figures walking, naked. Eve's mouth gaped like a wound in her upraised face. Her right arm wrapped her breasts, her left hand covered her sex. She was clasping the tender places of connection. Her shame was her body. That was her agony. Miranda stood, looking, absorbed by the horror and the shame. Eve's eyes, unseeing, wept. Her head was thrown back. The jaw gaped. 'There's an Oedipus there somewhere,' Miranda whispered to Louis, who was beside her again as she switched her gaze from Eve on to the figure of Adam. Adam held his hands to his face. His agony, the gesture signified, was mental.

'There used to be fig leaves', Louis said, 'before the restorers cleaned them off.'

'Adam's cock bounces forward jauntily enough,' Miranda said.

'You see that darker blue behind his back,' Louis said.

'No,' Miranda said. She had taken Louis's earlier silence for granted, and now he was displaying his customary enthusiasm. Had he been merely indifferent before, or shocked by her tears last night?

'See behind him, the sky's a darker colour. Then the rest is lighter.'

'Yes, I can.'

'Masaccio painted one section each day, you see, and of course it dried unevenly, but they'd never have left it that way, with that segment of darker blue. It would have been unprofessional. They would have blended it.' Louis made his way between the other visitors towards the fresco. Miranda followed. 'In fact,' Louis said, 'azurite didn't take to wet plaster very well. The pigment didn't impregnate. It had to be applied afterwards when the plaster was more or less dry. Now it's been cleaned that difference between the blues is obtrusive. One couldn't see it before, really. And the angel. That's wrong now.' Miranda looked at the banishing angel hovering over the figures. Louis was engrossed, talking with quiet intensity, almost to himself. 'Before the restoration the angel was never so prominent,' he murmured, still staring up at the 'Expulsion', 'it's dissipated all the tension and force that used to be drawn towards Adam.'

Miranda realised that Louis hardly noticed the figure of Eve. She turned away, moving back again through the crowd to the far wall. Louis went with her. 'See that face that looks out at us, in the group on the right of that fresco?' he said.

'Yes.'

'That's said to be Masaccio.'

'He looks like Tom Jones,' Miranda laughed irreverently. She was beginning to have the strangest feeling, as if a sort of vacancy was opening up somewhere along her spine.

Louis was already next to the fresco. Miranda went and stood beside him and noticed that the pigment in a patch of the lower folds of a cloak in the painting looked as if it had been recently scratched or etched on to the plastered surface. 'That's the way the Italians restore,' Louis said, peering at it. 'Minimal interference. No false cracks or any of that stuff the English do.'

'Hold me,' Miranda said lightly, turning to Louis. She felt she was falling, somewhere, down some space that opened up between her shoulder blades.

'Hold me,' Miranda said again, her voice down to a whisper. 'Tighter.'

'What is it?' Louis asked.

'I don't know.'

'What do you want?' His question irritated her. She stepped free of his embrace and wandered back into the crowd of onlookers and their Italian guide whose words she could not understand. As she looked back up at the despairing figures of Adam and Eve leaving Paradise she felt alone, as if she were about to fall. Their painted shadows marked the ground beneath their feet. They walked on solid ground. She looked towards Louis and saw that he was still on the other side of the room, and the sense that she was toppling or keeling over, passed. Someone walked in front of Louis. She caught sight of him again, looking oddly at her. She thought, he doesn't understand what's happening. Neither do I. He was walking towards her. He took her hand.

'Come on, let's go.'

She followed Louis to the narrow exit, passing the huge interior of the rest of the church unvisited beyond the red rope. Outside the rain had stopped and the grass and sky gleamed. Miranda said, 'I'd like to buy some postcards,' and started back towards the entrance.

Once inside she stood revolving the stand of postcards, flicking through them without interest until she felt sure of her bearings. She chose four cards. Then she spotted another and took it over to show to Louis, who was leafing through a book on the counter. 'I didn't notice this one in the chapel,' she said.

'It's a detail from St Peter distributing alms. There's a better one there,' Louis glanced past her and Miranda saw the same image reproduced as a poster fastened to the wall behind the till. It showed a woman in a dark dress, her hair concealed under a white rolled scarf, carrying a baby boy. The child's bare bottom rested on her arm. His expression was not clear, but the way he was turning towards something which had just caught his attention was unmistakable. His hands were in the air, letting go of the mother, yet staying close, seeking her out. The young mother was graceful, proud. Pain shaded her face and the whites of her eyes were startling.

Miranda bought a copy of the poster.

In the hotel bedroom early afternoon, they made love. Miranda said to Louis, who lay afterwards on the other bed, 'I suppose a lover's caress is like a mother's to a child.'

'Is that what I am?' he looked across the bed at her, his voice sharp with shock. 'Your lover?'

She realised her mistake. Obviously he wanted something more.

She suppressed a shudder. She got up and stood on the wooden steps and pulled the window closed.

Louis continued to lie there, hands clasped behind his head against the pillow. Miranda rummaged in the drawer for underclothes, embarrassed. She took her blouse from the wardrobe, pulled on her jeans. Louis's glasses caught the light and Miranda could not see his face.

That night Louis brushed his hand over her breasts, let it hover there, light as a breath of wind. And like the rustle of leaves, her desire lifted and breezed into life. She turned to him.

With Mick her breasts stayed dormant as if she were banked against another element, formless. But with Louis she was clearly herself, and aware of the power of being ten years older, her body open to his touch.

With Louis she felt she had hands, good for stroking and caressing, breasts also, lips, to be kissed and to kiss, a mouth, thighs, a belly, a vagina, as if she'd been restitched into a new body.

She turned and Louis stroked her belly in idle circles. Flick of a tail, like a fish. Confusion. She seemed to list over. As if knocked. Out of the mud below, tears rose, like bubbles to the surface.

'I miss Toby,' she heard herself repeat, as if it were someone else talking.

The next morning they drove to Lucca. Miranda slept in the car. They'd stayed awake half the night in the high-ceilinged room, Miranda never quite sure whether it was lust, love or loss that she was feeling. The emotions, whatever they were, left her drained. Louis too, she noticed that morning, had a wary look that she'd not seen before.

As soon as they entered the cathedral he grew excited again, his tone low and relentless. Miranda walked with him down the aisle, accustomed now to the acoustic resonance and chilling elegance of the church interiors.

Louis talked to her about the sculpture he was taking her to see, the Ilaria del Carretto Guinigi, Jacopo della Quercia's masterpiece, he said. Ilaria was sixteen years old when she died in childbirth. Her distraught husband, a feudal lord, commissioned a statue in her memory.

Miranda followed Louis past a set of pews into the murky gloom of the north transept. He inserted coins in a wall box.

The white marble figure of Ilaria lay, shining slightly, illuminated by a dim spotlight, along the top of a darker marble sarcophagus. 'A soul in marble,' Miranda said in wonder and awe as she gazed at the carving of the young woman. Her high buttoned gown was tied under the breasts, her rolled headdress was entwined with ribbon, her hands were crossed over the rise of her belly. A dog, its face turned towards its mistress, lay at her feet. The sides of the tomb were decorated by carvings of winged babies – *putti*, Louis called them.

'It was an absolute, a turning point in the history of art, as Masaccio's paintings were to be,' he said. He told her that the sculpture was also at the centre of a restoration controversy. Miranda must have surely read about it in the papers. A visiting art historian was taken to court after proclaiming that the Ilaria looked as if it had been cleaned with Ajax.

Miranda looked at the grey-blue veins in the marble, the soapy smoothness of the skin, the closed eyelids, the nose chipped at the end. 'Not quite like cleaning a sink,' she commented.

The light went out and Ilaria lay once again in shadow.

'Damn. I've run out of change.' Louis went to the near-by door and held it open to let in some daylight. Miranda walked around the tomb. Tiny pieces were broken off the folds of the gown. She felt caught by the effect of the carving, suspended between death and life. She thought of Ilaria – Hilary – the subject, who had died, and of the proximity of death in childbirth. Of that Louis knew nothing.

'Did the child live?' she asked Louis. He did not know. He walked off to a room on the other side of the cathedral, to find pictures of the Ilaria before it was cleaned.

Miranda left the sculpture. She passed a student in black leggings who was pacing out the distance between pillars and noticed, as the student made notations on her sketch pad, her carefully drawn plan of the cathedral floor. In front of the monstrous, ornate altar, Miranda stopped. She sat down on a pew. She felt the space of the cathedral vast around her and heard the mothlike fluttering of the voices of visitors. Memories started to wash over her in waves.

She remembered sitting on the bed in the hospital ward after Toby's birth, her breasts engorged, vein boned. Toby's birth had been a nightmare. Afterwards he'd been placed in an incubator and she had thought he might not live. She drew the curtains round the bed and held a suction cap over her nipple to pump her breasts for colostrum. An eighth of an inch of whitish, clearish liquid, a quarter of an inch, a half, collected in the attached bottle. Was that all? She gave the bottle to the nurse. By the end of the week she was told that Toby would live. He was put in the cot next to her, and she did not know what to do when he cried. The other mothers were along the corridor with their babies, watching a bathing lesson. She picked Toby up out of the cot. She held the light, breathing weight of him against her and walked up and down the whispering lino. She talked to him, the stranger, not quite a person, the bundled tiny being-in-waiting who was also utterly himself, telling him that he was safe with her, that there was snow, white and cold outside but that here, inside, he was warm and snug, dressed in his blue hospital baby gro, and with her. His face was still red, a new alive thing, so light, no weight at all. There. Still, he cried. Finally she left the ward and found a nurse. 'Feed him,' said the nurse. She returned to her cubicle, sat on her bed, half pulling the curtain around her. She undid the hooks and eyes at the front of her nursing bra and watched while his face turned instinctively towards her breast. She directed the nipple into his mouth. On he clamped. Her let-down reflex tugged under the areola, unexpectedly and uncontrollably. He sucked. His mouth slipped off and milk sprayed out like a garden sprinkler in all directions until he fastened his mouth around the nipple once again. She watched him. She watched his cheeks move with sucking. So that was what he wanted. To suck. Under the soft down of his hair, his scalp was covered in scabs where they had repeatedly tried to attach some instrument during the long labour of his birth.

Unaware of her surroundings Miranda continued to sit on the pew, thinking back to Toby's conception, when she had been out there in the darkness, beyond herself, beyond Mick, simultaneously in her body and out drifting, until a spin of light pierced the membrane of time and space. That extraordinary experience that she had forgotten until she discovered she was pregnant.

She looked around the cathedral. Over on the south side two men were leaving confessionals. A priest, watching from a doorway, withdrew. A man in a grey suit and a cheap red jumper kneeled in the pew in front of her and put his head in his hands. Miranda had an urge to kneel also, but she resisted.

Hands over her eyes. Louis. He was standing in the pew behind her. 'Hello, I've found it,' he said. She stood and said nothing. She walked with him across the cathedral to a room where a priest was keeping watch over the religious mementoes, postcards, guides and history books on sale. She had to think. She stood beside Louis and looked at the book he had found with photos of the Ilaria before its restoration. It was hard to tell whether the cleaning had destroyed anything. The marble was duller, perhaps, the creases blacker. She could look at no more pictures. She heard Louis continue to talk to her as they started to leave but she paid no attention to what he was saying until they passed a crucifixion in a large glass cubicle. 'That's supposed to be so holy that no restorer will touch it,' he said, sounding bored. He tried to clasp her hand but she withdrew it. She sensed his glance without returning it.

Out in the sun she felt relief and then knew she had decided. Louis was tedious. She had to leave him as soon as possible. She could hardly bear to stay. She wanted to see Toby again. She could not think about Mick. For the time being he did not matter.

Back at the car park a young gipsy woman was begging. 'What a way to earn a living,' Louis said, jiggling coins in his pocket. He unlocked the car door. By the time he started the engine the woman had walked away. He drove towards the exit. Next to the parking attendant's booth stood an African, a cluster of transparent plastic lighters bright as poppies in his hand. Louis paid the attendant the parking fee, and drove off. Neither of them, it seemed, wanted to buy a lighter.

On the drive back from Lucca there was something clinging, blaming, in Louis's looks at her. Did he realise that she was going to leave him?

Later, while Louis was in the bath, she picked up the phone and dialled London. Mick answered. He put Toby on and she heard his baby voice say 'hello', go silent, then say, 'Where find Miranda?'

She switched off the light and lay back. She felt something like a warmth or a presence, in the darkened room. She could not abandon motherhood, slough it off like an unwanted skin, and walk into another life.

She was left with a residue of feeling, a faint imprint that seemed to be nothing but the absence of terror, and she thought the feeling must vanish altogether but it did not. She thought, sleepily, that what she felt was like faith, faith being whatever she might make of it. Whatever. Including motherhood. She heard Louis let out the bath water.

From the plane window on the way back she saw the Alps

piercing up through the clouds and on the horizon, caught by the slant of the sun, a swimming God sculpted in cumulo-nimbus. She was careful not to crush the poster of the mother holding her child that lay rolled and wrapped in plastic at her feet.

❧ *The Means of Escape*

PENELOPE FITZGERALD

St George's Church, Hobart, stands high above Battery Point and the harbour. Inside, it looks strange and must always have done so, although (at the time I'm speaking of) it didn't have the blue, pink and yellow-patterned stained glass that you see there now. That was ordered from a German firm in 1875. But St George's has always had the sarcophagus-shaped windows which the architect had thought Egyptian and therefore appropriate (St George is said to have been an Egyptian saint). They give you the curious impression, as you cross the threshold, of entering a tomb.

In 1852, before the organ was installed, the church used to face east, and music was provided by a seraphine. The seraphine was built, and indeed invented, by a Mr Ellard, formerly of Dublin, now a resident of Hobart. He intended it to suggest the angelic choir, although the singing voices at his disposal – the surveyor general, the naval chaplain, the harbourmaster and their staffs – were for the most part male. Who was able to play the seraphine? Only, at first, Mr Ellard's daughter, Mrs Logan, who seems to have got £20 a year for doing so, the same fee as the clerk and the sexton. When Mrs Logan began to feel the task was too much for her – the seraphine needs continuous pumping – she instructed Alice Godley, the rector's daughter.

Hobart stands 'south of no north', between snowy Mount Wellington and the river Derwent, running down over steps and promontories to the harbour's bitterly cold water. You get all the winds that blow. The next stop to the south is the limit of the Antarctic drift ice. When Alice came up to practise the hymns she had to unlock the outer storm door, made of Huon pine, and the inner door, also a storm door, and drag them shut again.

The seraphine stood on its own square of Axminster carpet in the transept. Outside (at the time I'm speaking of) it was a bright afternoon, but inside St George's there was that mixture of light and inky darkness which suggests that from the darkness something may be about to move. It was difficult, for instance, to distinguish whether among the black-painted pews, at some distance away, there was or wasn't some person or object rising above the level of the seats. Alice liked to read mystery stories, when she could get hold of them, and the thought struck her now, 'The form of a man is advancing from the shadows.'

If it had been ten years ago, when she was still a schoolgirl, she might have shrieked out, because at that time there were said to be bolters and escaped convicts from Port Arthur on the loose everywhere. The constabulary hadn't been put on to them. Now there were only a few names of runaways, perhaps twenty, posted up on the notice boards outside Government House.

'I did not know that anyone was in the church,' she said. 'It is kept locked. I am the organist. Perhaps I can assist you?'

A rancid stench, not likely from someone who wanted to be shown round the church, came towards her up the aisle. The shape, too, seemed wrong. But that, she saw, was because the head was hidden in some kind of sack like a butchered animal, or, since it had eyeholes, more like a man about to be hung.

'Yes,' he said, 'you can be of assistance to me.'

'I think now that I can't be,' she said, picking up her music case. 'No nearer,' she added distinctly.

He stood still, but said, 'We shall have to get to know one another better.' And then, 'I am an educated man. You may try me out if you like, in Latin and some Greek. I have come from Port Arthur. I was a poisoner.'

'I should not have thought you were old enough to be married.'

'I never said I poisoned my wife!' he cried.

'Were you innocent, then?'

'You women think that everyone in gaol is innocent. No, I'm not innocent, but I was wrongly incriminated. I never lifted a hand. They criminated me on false witness.'

'I don't know about lifting a hand,' she said. 'You mentioned that you were a poisoner.'

'My aim in saying that was to frighten you,' he said. 'But that is no longer my aim at the moment.'

It had been her intention to walk straight out of the church, managing the doors as quickly as she could, and on no account looking back at him, since she believed that with a man of bad character, as with a horse, the best thing was to show no emotion whatever. He, however, moved round through the pews in such a way as to block her way.

He told her that the name he went by, which was not his given name, was Savage. He had escaped from the Model Penitentiary. He had a knife with him, and had thought at first to cut her throat, but had seen almost at once that the young lady was not on the cross. He had got into the church tower (which was half finished, but no assigned labour could be found to work on it at the moment) through the gaps left in the brickwork. Before he could ask for food she told him firmly that she herself could get him none. Her father was the incumbent, and the most generous of men, but at the Rectory they had to keep very careful count of everything, because charity was given out at the door every Tuesday and Thursday evening. She might be able to bring him the spent tea-leaves, which were always kept, and he could mash them again if he could find warm water.

'That's a sweet touch!' he said. 'Spent tea-leaves!'

'It is all I can do now, but I have a friend – I may perhaps be able to do more later. However, you can't stay here beyond tomorrow.'

'I don't know what day it is now.'

'It is Wednesday, the twelfth of November.'

'Then *Constancy* is still in harbour.'

'How do you know that?'

It was all they did know, for certain, in the penitentiary. There was a rule of absolute silence, but the sailing lists were passed secretly between those who could read, and memorised from them by those who could not.

'*Constancy* is a converted collier, carrying cargo and a hundred and fifty passengers, laying at Franklin Wharf. I am entrusting you with my secret intention, which is to stow on her to Portsmouth, or as far at least as Cape Town.'

He was wearing grey felon's slops. At this point he took off his hood, and stood wringing it round and round in his hands, as though he was trying to wash it.

Alice looked at him directly for the first time.

'I shall need a change of clothing, ma'am.'

'You may call me "Miss Alice",' she said.

At the prompting of some sound, or imaginary sound, he retreated and vanished up the dark gap, partly boarded up, of the staircase to the tower. That which had been on his head was left in a heap on the pew. Alice took it up and put it into her music case, pulling the strap tight.

She was lucky in having a friend very much to her own mind, Aggie, the daughter of the people who ran Shuckburgh's Hotel; Aggie Shuckburgh, in fact.

'He might have cut your throat, did you think of that?'

'He thought better of it,' said Alice.

'What I should like to know is this: why didn't you go straight to your father, or to Colonel Johnson at the Constabulary? I don't wish you to answer me at once, because it mightn't be the truth. But tell me this: would you have acted in the same manner, if it had been a woman hiding in the church?' Alice was silent, and Aggie asked, 'Did a sudden strong warmth spring up between the two of you?'

'I think that it did.'

No help for it, then, Aggie thought. 'He'll be hard put to it, I'm afraid. There's no water in the tower, unless the last lot of builders left a pailful, and there's certainly no dunny.' But Alice thought he might slip out by night. 'That is what I should do myself, in his place.' She explained that Savage was an intelligent man, and that he intended to stow away on *Constancy*.

'My dear, you're not thinking of following him?'

'I'm not thinking at all,' said Alice.

They were in the hotel, checking the clean linen. So many tablecloths, so many aprons, kitchen, so many aprons, dining room, so many pillow shams. They hardly ever talked without working. They knew their duties to both their families.

Shuckburgh's had its own warehouse and bond store on the harbour front. Aggie would find an opportunity to draw out, not any of the imported goods, but at least a ration of tea and bacon. Then they could see about getting it up to the church.

'As long as you didn't imagine it, Alice!'

Alice took her arm. 'Forty-five!'

They had settled on the age of forty-five to go irredeemably cranky. They might start imagining anything they liked then. The whole parish, indeed the whole neighbourhood, thought that they were cranky already, in any case, not to get settled, Aggie in particular, with all the opportunities that came her way in the hotel trade.

'He left this behind,' said Alice, opening her music case, which let fly a feral odour. She pulled out the sacking mask, with its slits, like a mourning pierrot's, for eyes.

'Do they make them wear those?'

'I've heard Father speak about them often. They wear them every time they go out of their cells. They're part of the new system, they have to prove their worth. With the masks on, none of the other prisoners can tell who a man is, and he can't tell who they are. He mustn't speak either, and that drives a man into himself, so that he's alone with the Lord, and can't help but think over his wrongdoing and repent. I never saw one of them before today, though.'

'It's got a number on it,' said Aggie, not going so far as to touch it. 'I dare say they put them to do their own laundry.'

At the Rectory there were five people sitting down already to the four o'clock dinner. Next to her father was a guest, the visiting preacher; next to him, was Mrs Watson, the housekeeper. She had come to Van Diemen's Land with a seven-year sentence, and now had her ticket of leave. Assigned servants usually ate in the backhouse, but in the Rector's household all were part of the same family. Then, the Lukes. They were penniless immigrants (his papers had Mr Luke down as a scene-painter, but there was no theatre in Hobart). He had been staying, with his wife, for a considerable time.

Alice asked them all to excuse her for a moment while she went up to her room. Once there, she lit a piece of candle and burned the lice off the seams of the mask. She put it over her head. It did not disarrange her hair, the neat smooth hair of a minister's daughter, always presentable on any occasion. But the eyeholes came too low down, so that she could see nothing and stood there in stifling darkness. She asked herself, 'Wherein have I sinned?'

Her father, who never raised his voice, called from downstairs, 'My dear, we are waiting.' She took off the mask, folded it, and put it in the hamper where she kept her woollen stockings.

After grace they ate red snapper, boiled mutton and bread pudding, no vegetables. In England the Reverend Alfred Godley had kept a good kitchen garden, but so far he had not been able to get either leeks or cabbages going in the thin earth round Battery Point.

Mr Luke hoped that Miss Alice had found her time at the instrument well spent.

'I could not get much done,' she answered. 'I was interrupted.'

'Ah, it's a sad thing for a performer to be interrupted. The concentration of the mind is gone. "When the lamp is shattered . . ."'

'That is not what I felt at all,' said Alice.

'You are too modest to admit it.'

'I have been thinking, Father,' said Alice, 'that since Mr Luke cares so much for music, it would be a good thing for him to try the seraphine himself. Then if by any chance I had to go away, you would be sure of a replacement.'

'You speak as if my wife and I should be here always,' cried Mr Luke.

Nobody made any comment on this – certainly not Mrs Luke, who passed her days in a kind of incredulous stupor. How could it be that she was sitting here eating bread pudding some twelve thousand miles from Clerkenwell, where she had spent all the rest of her life? The Rector's attention had been drawn away by the visiting preacher, who had taken out a copy of the *Hobart Town Daily Courier*, and was reading aloud a paragraph which announced his arrival from Melbourne. 'Bringing your welcome with you,' the Rector exclaimed. 'I am glad the *Courier* noted it.' – 'Oh, they would not have done,' said the preacher, 'but I make it my practice to call in at the principal newspaper offices wherever I go, and make myself known with a few friendly words. In that way, if the editor has nothing of great moment to fill up his sheet, which is frequently the case, it is more than likely that he will include something about my witness.' He had come on a not very successful mission to pray that gold would never be discovered in Van Diemen's Land, as it had been on the mainland, bringing with it the occasion of new temptations.

After the dishes were cleared Alice said she was going back for a while to Aggie's, but would, of course, be home before dark. Mr Luke, while his wife sat on with half-closed eyes, came out to the back kitchen and asked Mrs Watson, who was at the sink, whether he could make himself useful by pumping up some more water.

'No,' said Mrs Watson.

Mr Luke persevered. 'I believe you to have had considerable experience of life. Now, I find Miss Alice charming, but somewhat difficult to understand. Will you tell me something about her?'

'No.'

Mrs Watson was, at the best of times, a very silent woman, whose life had been an unfortunate one. She had lost three children before being transported, and could not now remember what they had been called. Alice, however, did not altogether believe this, as she had met other women who thought it unlucky to name their dead children. Mrs Watson had certainly been out of luck with her third, a baby, who had been left in the charge of a little girl of ten, a neighbour's daughter, who acted as nursemaid for fourpence a week. How the house came to catch fire was not known. It was a flash fire. Mrs Watson was out at work. The man she lived with was in the house, but he was very drunk, and doing – she supposed – the best he could under the circumstances, he pitched both the neighbour's girl and the baby out of the window. The coroner had said that it might just as well have been a Punch and Judy show. 'Try to think no more about it,' Alice advised her. As chance would have it, Mrs Watson had been taken up only a week later for thieving. She had tried to throw herself in the river, but the traps had pulled her out again.

On arrival in Hobart she had been sent to the Female Factory, and later, after a year's steady conduct, to the Hiring Depot where employers could select a pass-holder. That was how, several years ago, she had fetched up at the Rectory. Alice had taught her to write and read, and had given her (as employers were required to do in any case) a copy of the Bible. She handed over the book with a kiss. On the flyleaf she had copied out a verse from Hosea – 'Say to your sister, *Ruhaman*, you have obtained mercy.'

Mrs Watson had no documents which indicated her age, and her pale face was not so much seamed or lined as knocked, apparently, out of the true by a random blow which might have been time or chance. Perhaps she had always looked like that. Although she said nothing by way of thanks at the time, it was evident, as the months went by, that she had transferred the weight of unexpected affection which is one of a woman's greatest inconveniences on to Miss Alice. This was clear partly from the way she occasionally caught hold of Alice's hand and held it for a while, and from her imitation, sometimes unconsciously grotesque, of Alice's rapid walk and her way of doing things about the house.

Aggie had the tea, the bacon, the plum jam, and, on her own initiative, had added a roll of tobacco. This was the only item from the bond store and perhaps should have been left alone, but neither of the girls had ever met or heard of a man who didn't smoke or chew tobacco if he had the opportunity. They knew that on Norfolk Island and at Port Arthur the convicts sometimes killed for tobacco.

They had a note of the exact cash value of what was taken. Alice would repay the amount to Shuckburgh's Hotel from the money she earned from giving music lessons. (She had always refused to take a fee for playing the seraphine at St George's.) But what of truth's claim, what of honesty's? Well, Alice would leave, say, a hundred and twenty days for *Constancy* to reach Portsmouth. Then she would go to her father.

'What will you say to him?' Aggie asked.

'I shall tell him that I have stolen and lied, and caused my friend to steal and lie.'

'Yes, but that was all in the name of the corporeal mercies. You felt pity for this man, who had been a prisoner, and was alone in the wide world.'

'I am not sure that what I feel is pity.'

Certainly the two of them must have been seen through the shining front windows of the new terraced houses on their way up to the church. Certainly they were seen with their handcart, but this was associated with parish magazines and requests for a subscription to something or other, so that at the sight of it the watchers left their windows. At the top of the rise Aggie, who was longing to have a look at Alice's lag, said, 'I'll not come in with you.'

'But, Aggie, you've done so much, and you'll want to see his face.'

'I do want to see his face, but I'm keeping myself in check. That's what forms the character, keeping yourself in check at times.'

'Your character is formed already, Aggie.'

'Sakes, Alice, do you want me to come in with you?'

'No.'

'Mr Savage,' she called out decisively.

'I am just behind you.'

Without turning round, she counted out the packages in their stout wrappings of whitish paper. He did not take them, not even the tobacco, but said, 'I have been watching you and the other young lady from the tower.'

'This situation can't continue,' said Alice. 'There is the regular Moonah Men's prayer meeting on Friday.'

'I shall make a run for it tomorrow night,' said Savage, 'but I need women's clothing. I am not of heavy build. The flesh came off me at Port Arthur, one way and another. Can you furnish me?'

'I must not bring women's clothes to the church,' said Alice. 'St Paul forbids it.' But she had often felt that she was losing patience with St Paul.

'If he won't let you come to me, I must come to you,' said Savage.

'You mean to my father's house?'

'Tell me the way exactly, Miss Alice, and which your room is. As soon as the time's right, I will knock twice on your window.'

'You will not knock on it once,' said Alice. 'I don't sleep on the ground floor.'

'Does your room face the sea?'

'No, I don't care to look at the sea. My window looks on to the Derwent, up the river valley to the north-west.'

Now that she was looking at him he put his two thumbs and forefingers together in a sign which she had understood and indeed used herself ever since she was a child. It meant *I give you my whole heart.*

'I should have thought you might have wanted to know what I was going to do when I reached England,' he said.

'I do know. You'll be found out, taken up and committed to Pentonville as an escaped felon.'

'Only give me time, Miss Alice, and I will send for you.'

In defiance of any misfortune that might come to him, he would send her the needful money for her fare and his address, once he had a home for her, in England.

'Wait and trust, give me time, and I will send for you.'

In low-built, shipshape Battery Point the Rectory was unusual in being three storeys high, but it had been smartly designed with ironwork Trafalgar balconies, and the garden had been planted with English roses as well as daisy bushes and silver wattle. It was the Rector's kindheartedness which had made it take on the appearance of a human warren. Alice's small room, as she had told Savage, looked out on to the river. Next to her, on that side of the house, was the visiting preacher's room, always called, as in the story of Elijah, the prophet's chamber. The Lukes faced the sea, and the Rector had retreated to what had once been his study. Mrs Watson slept at the back, over the wash-house, which projected from the kitchen. Above were the box-rooms, all inhabited by a changing population of no-hopers, thrown out of work by the depression of the 1840s. These people did not eat at the Rectory – they went to the Colonial Families' Charitable on Knopwood Street – but their washing and their poultry had given the grass plot the air of a seedy encampment, ready to surrender at the first emergency.

Alice did not undress the following night, but lay down in her white blouse and waist. One of her four shawls and one of her three skirts lay folded over the back of the sewing chair. At first she lay there and smiled, then almost laughed out loud at the notion of Savage, like a mummer in a Christmas pantomine, struggling down the Battery steps and on to the wharves under the starlight in her nankeen petticoat. Then she ceased smiling, partly because she felt the unkindness of it, partly because of her perplexity as to why he needed to make this very last part of his run in skirts. Did he have in mind to set sail as a woman?

She let her thoughts run free. She knew perfectly well that Savage, after years of enforced solitude, during which he had been afforded no prospect of a woman's love, was unlikely to be coming to her room just for a bundle of clothes. If he wanted to get to bed her, what then, ought she to raise the house? She imagined calling out (though not until he was gone), and her door opening, and the bare shanks of the rescuers jostling in in their nightshirts – the visiting preacher, Mr Luke, her father, the upstairs lodgers – and she prayed for grace. She thought of the forgiven – Rahab, the harlot of Jericho, the wife of Hosea who had been a prostitute, Mary Magdalene, Mrs Walker who had cohabited with a drunken man.

You may call me Miss Alice.

I will send for you.

You could not hear St George's clock from the Rectory. She marked the hours from the clock at Government House on the waterfront. It had been built by convict labour and intended first of all as the Customs House. It was now three o'clock. The *Constancy* sailed at first light.

Give me time and I will send for you.

If he had been seen leaving the church, and arrested, they would surely have come to tell the Rector. If he had missed the way to the Rectory and been caught wandering in the streets, then no one else was to blame but herself. I should have brought him straight home with me. He should have obtained mercy. I should have called out aloud to every one of them – look at him, this is the man who will send for me.

The first time she heard a tap at the window she lay still, thinking, 'He may look for me if he chooses.' It was nothing, there was no one there. The second and third times, at which she got up and crossed the cold floor, were also nothing.

Alice, however, did receive a letter from Savage (he still gave himself that name). It arrived about eight months later, and had been despatched from Portsmouth. By that time she was exceedingly busy, since Mrs Watson had left the Rectory, and had not been replaced.

Honoured Miss Alice,

I think it only proper to do Justice to Myself, by telling you the Circumstances which took place on the 12 of November Last Year. In the First Place, I shall not forget your Kindness. Even when I go down to the Dust, as we all shall do so, a Spark will proclaim, that Miss Alice Godley Relieved me in my Distress.

Having got to the Presbittery in accordance with your Directions, I made sure first of your Room, facing North West, and got up the House the handiest way, by scaleing the Wash-house Roof, intending to make the Circuit of the House by means of the Ballcony and its varse Quantity of creepers. But I was made to Pause at once by a Window opening and an Ivory Form leaning out, and a Woman's Voice suggesting a natural Proceeding between us, which there is no need to particularise. When we had done our business, she said further, You may call me Mrs Watson, tho it is not my Name. – I said to her, I am come here in search of Woman's Clothing. I am a convict on the bolt, and it is my intention to conceal myself on Constancy, laying at Franklyn Wharf. She replied immediately, 'I can Furnish you, and indeed I can see No Reason, why I should not Accompany you.'

This letter of Savage's in its complete form, is now, like so many memorials of convict days, in the National Library of Tasmania, in Hobart. There is no word in it to Alice Godley from Mrs Watson herself. It would seem that like many people who became literate later in life she read a great deal – the Bible in particular – but never took much to writing, and tended to mistrust it. In consequence her motives for doing what she did – which, taking into account her intense affection for Alice, must have been complex enough – were never set down, and can only be guessed at.

∽ Land's End

GARY INDIANA

There was a man who loved a sailor, but the sailor loved the sea. This is what a little girl of the town sings as she walks along the sea-wall promenade. Postcards of the shore view from the promenade, the wild waves spewing and shattering against the large prehistoric stones along the shore, are available at Mrs Duffy's tobacco shop on Nelson Avenue, named for Admiral, Lord Nelson, who once took a leak in a spittoon belonging to old Lucy Abernthnot's grandmother.

As in the movies, the landscape's a given: the town, perched on the Western Cliffs, above the roiling, churning, treacherous grey jello of the sea, with the harbour further down the shore, a park edged with rain trees and poplars encompassing the stone church and the graveyard, a damp, drizzling landscape subject to low clouds and epidemics of pneumonia, heavy fogs, arthritic flare-ups, and shipwrecks. The village of narrow, septic, serpentine streets, some of them still cobbled, contains a number of rustic inns, fish and chip shops, antique stores, second-hand booksellers, and a plethora of retirees, many of them fishermen, and their gravid, thrifty wives.

At the small, private insanity clinic run by Dr John Pretorius, a male patient in his mid-fifties has begun to exhibit altogether new symptoms of delusion. Renfield is a former classics scholar who, one especially drenched and lowering afternoon, sent his wife to the next world with a modicum of fuss and bother, his method a swift shove down the basement stairs of their semi-detached. Renfield's now obsessed by a religious fad, something out of Hinduism if Pretorius is not mistaken, and claims that each living organism has a soul. He's started a large collection of pet flies, attracting the little beasts with sugar.

Everyone knows the disturbing recent events that've shaken the town's placid, moist, deliquescent demeanour. The breaking-up of the commercial brigantine *Marlene* on the rocks below the cliffs, on a night of storm and implacable mists, the grotesque discovery of Captain Beauregard Slyme-Fitzpatrick, mummified by the salt spray, his face in death a rictus of horror, handcuffed to the steering wheel, the eerie absence of the crew, the curious ship's log of which the local authorities can make neither head nor tail, as it describes some variety of supernatural phenomena aboard the *Marlene* (though it has been rumoured that Captain Slyme-Fitzpatrick dabbled in mesmerism and table-tapping), the thirty-odd boxes of dirt which have since been requisitioned by Musk, Smegma & Cunningham, solicitors, and the large, ungovernable German shepherd dog that sprang from below deck as the wreckage was towed into shore and bolted off into the countryside. A number of local canines have been mauled and maimed on their evening prowls, presumably by this ship's stray, and the local ASPCA is doing its all to locate and restrain the animal.

In a boarding house where the widow Doris Humphreys and her celebrated treacle tarts preside over twelve mostly unoccupied rooms and a breakfast table groaning with arcane meats and her other speciality, 'stiff breads', the writer Dennis Stoker gazes up at midnight from a letter on blue airmail paper he received earlier in the day from Seth Myers, currently in Bombay. Framed in his window, the view extends beyond the miserable running puddle of the town's nameless river, into the verdant but sombre churchyard, its huddled gravestones chalky in the moonlight. In his mind's eye Dennis caresses Seth's grey-brown skin, something he's never had the nerve to do in real life, explores with his tongue Seth's dark, expressive lips. Thus far their friendship has been strictly that, an exchange of daily irritations and bits of news. Seth's writing a book on India, Dennis is writing one on the Dullwich Ripper, a still-at-large maniac who preys on adolescent boys in the near-by city of Dullwich. Can he love me, Dennis wonders, where I'm so much older than him, we've so much in common on the one hand, on the other hand he's never seemed much interested in a physical relationship, what on earth is going on over there, that looks like Paul floating around in the cemetery, what's that dark shape, oh dear.

In galoshes and a raincoat from GAP, Dennis braves the silty local mud along the riverbank, aided by a sleekly designed but dim flashlight he happened to have in his luggage, crosses the rickety bridge of woven liana vines and worm-eaten planks over the anonymous weather-tossed river, and sloshes up the opposite bank. The rain is a needlelike downpour of soft water, the kind that gets into everything. It's fearsome dark in the churchyard, and when he spots what looks like the milky white form of Paul, his new acquaintance from the boarding house, it looks as though a blurry figure in evening clothes has just detached himself from the young man and left him lying spread-eagled on one of the carved ferro-concrete benches, wearing a dazed expression of mindless rapture. Dennis rushes to Paul's side as the dark figure scurries into the inkblack woods surrounding the churchyard.

Paul is groggy and almost naked, wearing only a sopping tee-shirt and a pair of sodden underpants: dripping wet, his shaggy black hair clinging to his skull, he mutters something about valium while Dennis leads him back to the boarding house, stopping to place his own expensive Nikes on Paul's bare feet. Back at Mrs Humphreys, he washes and dries the semi-comatose Paul and settles him under the eiderdown in the boy's room, wondering where on earth Marcus, Paul's blazingly handsome but aloof boyfriend, has got himself off to.

Pretorius wakes to the howling of a dog. He's amazed and a little pissed that the noise has roused him from a seven-drop tincture of laudanum sleep, then hears Barney, the Jamaican orderly, pounding at his bedroom door. It's Renfield again, the giant Rastafarian exclaims, his powerful body wreathed in the scent of ganja. That Renfield a crazy son of a bitch. Pretorius throws on a housecoat and follows Barney into the east wing and Renfield's padded cell. Barney throws the door open. See what I'm saying? That fool even more further out of his mind.

It's true. Renfield huddles in a corner, teeth chattering, eyes popping from his head, stuffing handfuls of dead flies into his mouth and wailing like a lunatic, which, of course, he is. But things have gotten worse, Pretorius muses, ever since the wreckage of the *Marlene* and the leasing out of the old Bridwell manor house across the way. Renfield's taken to singing hymns, always an ominous development, and prattling of Him who is about to Come. He orders Barney, whose horror of all things anal Pretorius considers a surmountable phobia, immediately to administer an enema spiked with laudanum.

As Barney inserts the nozzle of the enema bag, Pretorius questions Renfield, whose agitation has subsided: Who is this Him you keep referring to? Who is He? You know who He is, Renfield cackles with his usual maddening insinuation. The Big Man. The Chief. You'll find out. One of these days. Yes, doctor, you're in for quite a tasty little surprise once He gets here. He's promised me things, Renfield teases in a feline voice. Big things. What things, Pretorius asks, his clinician's curiosity poking through the clouds of laudanum. Oh, Renfield singsongs, just . . . things, things you wouldn't know a thing about. Just then, to Pretorius's great disgust and Barney's obvious horror, the doped enema works its magic.

Are you all right, Dennis asks Paul, whom he's discovered still lying in bed at eleven in the morning. The youth's face is alarmingly pale. Paul attempts a carefree smile. I feel weak, he declares. You were sleepwalking, Dennis tells him, taking one of his hands between his. Where's Marcus, anyway? Oh, yawns Paul, he's got all these job interviews in Dullwich, he stayed overnight. Do you often walk in your sleep? No, says Paul, after a long silence, only since we came here. I've had such disturbing dreams. Dreams? Dennis says. What kind of dreams? Oh, odd dreams, in which I'm gliding along over the earth, my feet aren't touching the ground, I'm propelled by some ... dark force, it could be a man in a very old and dusty tuxedo that looks like someone dropped talcum powder on it, and in his lapel he's got a gardenia, except the gardenia's actually made of a thousand tiny insects who adopt the form of a gardenia for camouflage, and the man's doing something with his hands. What's he doing? He's wringing the neck of a chicken, I think. But he also could be playing solitaire. In the dream, I think he's doing both. I mean when I'm inside the dream there's no discrepancy or contradiction about it, it makes sense that's what he'd be doing.

Dennis was fighting his own sleepiness by this time, since Paul's dream seemed to lead nowhere and bored him, besides. He had no interest in explaining the shadow drama out there on the moor or the heath or whatever it was called. Paul had obviously picked up a piece of trade down at the harbour, God knew it was easy enough to do, stand them a couple dozen lagers in the Whore of Dorset Inn and offer them five or six bob or whatever the currency was, and you could be more or less certain of making the bottom rump of the two-backed beast in some piss-smelling sylvan glade they all frequented far into the morning. The only question was, where had Paul put all his clothing to make it seem he had walked in his sleep.

He knew there were Problems between Paul and Marcus, Problems which in no way had any weight with him, for his main job now was to finger the Dullwich Ripper before the police did, and perhaps more importantly to seduce Seth with letters that made it plain, but only if interpreted in a certain light, that the thought of Seth's body made him crazy at night, though the letters would not hint that he was crazy enough to consider a roll in the hay with the cute kid down the hall Chez Humphreys. Suddenly the Problems between Paul and Marcus took on relevance in Dennis's mind.

No clues so far to the Ripper's identity. Some claim it's the tubby German proprietor of the Whore of Dorset, though they say down at the Bucket of Lard that Lord Davies, who's hardly ever at his manor house, came down with a group of horsemen fifteen days ago, at the commencement of the ghastly crimes going on up in Dullwich, and furthermore Horrocks, the insurance adjuster, says that the children or young boys or whatever they were all had their throats ripped out, which indicates hunters, or hunter's dogs, over at the Lucky Pint it's three with their throats ripped out and three others with their faces slashed to bits, at the Slobbering Duke they say only two ripped-out throats, three faces slashed, while the sixth was throttled with a Christian Dior tie, in any case local suspicion has settled on Lord Davies as the most likely criminal culprit, Lord Davies or one of his gin-swilling High Almighty ruling-class friends, they all went to school together, Eton or Harrow or Her Majesty's Penitentiary, hard to tell, one school of thought proclaims that Lord Davies's dissipation is written all over his face, at the Bucket of Lard it's widely held that Lord Davies is secretly a Jew and feasts on the blood of adolescents, though really, as the German at the Whore of Dorset tells everyone loudly and *ad infinitum*, the Jews generally feast on the blood of infants, only at the Lucky Pint does the German-at-the-Whore-of-Dorset-as-the-Ripper theory seem to hold any water, perhaps because Mellors, the gamekeeper on the Sex Pistols' Estate, got in a terrible row with Lord Davies a year ago last autumn over rabbits, the blood of which is supposed to be retained for use in the annual stone-turning pageant held in the village, which Lord Davies dismisses as an out-of-date custom and therefore refuses to bleed the rabbit carcasses shot by him and his High Almighty ruling-class friends, whereas Mellors and other working-class lads from the village view the stone-turning pageant as a contest of virility and hence look forward to it every year. It's remarkable, Dennis thinks, that these customs dating back to the Druids or the Norman Conquest, whichever was further back, persist right into the modern era. If Seth would only give a hint in his letters, some sign. But perhaps the mere fact of getting these letters is proof enough. On the other hand, perhaps not.

Doris Humphreys was knitting a shawl or sweater or something that would one day be large enough to cover the entire village. She had started it after her husband perished at sea twenty years ago. It now dominated her once-airy salon at the front of the house, the side facing the street rather than the river embankment, and it was mostly a deathly aubergine in colour but there were bits of orange and eau-de-nil in it too, the thing had accumulated in great piles that had to be folded over on to each other, but then that'd gotten too cramped, so parts of it were placed in the hall closet, which meant you had really always to step over Mrs Humphreys's shawl on your way to the dining room, the garment or revenge on passing time or whatever it was kept expanding and billowing through the house, infiltrating the unrented rooms, wrapping itself around lamps and china closets and sticks of shabby sea-bitten furniture, at times Paul could feel the tissue-like layers of the shawl engulfing him in his sleep, like thousands of caressing insects, mainly benign insects like moths, benign that is to him rather than to Mrs Humphreys's scarf, shawl, thingamajig, in the dream the moths had already made some inroads on it, and it always felt as though Marcus had returned, altered in some appealing yet repulsive way, though it crossed his mind that Marcus was seeing someone in Dullwich, perhaps more than one person if past performance were anything to go by, Paul adored Marcus but he really was a whore, or the next best thing to a whore, a slut, with his saucy lips and limpid eyes of a Hummel figurine, really he wouldn't even think about Dennis if Marcus were around, Dennis or the others.

In fact Paul had been thinking about many young men in the village, most of them louts, but louts with a certain *je ne sais quoi*, nature had given them little in the way of faces but their bodies, which smelt like country cheese and cow manure, had taken from the rigours of their miserable backgrounds the look of protean energy and unmistakable, indeed volcanic, sexual frustration. They had read Lawrence and Jackie Collins and they knew about fiery loins. The young women of the village wanted marriage and nothing else, but many of them managed to get something else on Saturday nights in the alleyway behind the Whore of Dorset, particularly each year in the wake of the stone-turning pageant, often resulting a few months later in marriage if not a wedding ring. Life with one of these men would be brutal, as would the single night Paul entertained in his reveries.

Now he's raising spiders, Barney informs Dr Pretorius. Pretorius has just injected himself and really doesn't see what difference it makes, flies or spiders, the man's a *tragedian*, Pretorius tells himself, making much ado about nothing whatever. Flies, spiders – well, Renfield's moving up the food chain. Once he gets up to larger animals, as Pretorius well knows from his study of zoophagy, there will be far too much commotion to keep Renfield on the premises. It will have to be Broadmoor for Renfield, no doubt about it. Unpleasant fellow. Always impugning my knowledge of the classics and trying to stump me with questions about Hume's theory of sensory perception I believe it is. And then chewing up those files with such uninhibited gusto. Something sort of winning about that part, medically speaking. God, I feel good. Pity Barney won't make himself more comfortable on these occasions rather than just stand there yearning for a morphine fix.

Dennis? Am I bothering you? No? Oh, good. Last night – it was awfully sweet of you to get me off that heath. Yes, it's heath, I should know, I – well, anyway, it's been on my mind all day to thank you properly. Listen, Dennis says, you're making me embarrassed. I only thought you'd catch your death out there in this vicious weather. Dennis idly rummages through the closet, admiring Marcus's extensive wardrobe, not for the first time. Shortly before Marcus's departure for Dullwich, the three of them whiled away a damp afternoon trying on one another's clothes. That seems long ago and far away to Dennis now. Is a bit sodden, says Paul. At least it's warm in this dump. Are you as sick of treacle tart as I am? How on earth did she win a prize for those pruney monstrosities?

Dennis covers the letter to Seth with a copy of The Satanic Bible he's been perusing in search of a plausible lead in the Ripper business. Paul's nervous prattle confirms Dennis's idea that Paul wants to make it with him, passionately, regardless of Seth, regardless of Marcus, wants Dennis's hard, eager thrusts on

Mrs Humphreys's soft, faintly cat-pissy canopied guest bed. How can one be faithful to an ideal that hasn't come to pass? It could be messy, though. How could he look Marcus in the eye afterwards? Easy, Dennis thinks. There are so many ways to dissemble a love affair. And lots of other affairs too. The question is, can Paul restrain himself from flaunting it in Marcus's face if they start fighting again? Paul's not exactly a subtle person. And if he tells him beforehand that he must never, ever inform Marcus about what they're going to do, will have done, rather, once they're finished doing it, that means having to verbalise everything in advance and Dennis hates doing that. He likes going into things with his eyes closed.

Inspector Sweeney ate with relish the inner organs of beasts and fowls, but the autopsy photos laid before him on the snotgreen blotter of his telephone desk put him right off his feed. Innocent youths snuffled out before the prime of life, necks mangled with some arcane instrument wielded by an archfiend the likes of whom had not been spotted around Dullwich since the days of the nauseating Rushton Hall Homicides. There, too, the victims had been all working class, comely, apparently dimwitted and lubricious youths, that for a fantasy or trick of fame went to their graves like beds, ensorcelled by the lisping promises of the deranged Lord Catheter of Land's End. Sweeney vividly recalled how they had run the demented Catheter to earth, the hounds innervated by a shred of the maniac's foundation garments the final victim, young Dick Clotho of Burton upon Trent, had managed to tear off with his teeth in his penultimate throes.

He uses some sort of bladed meat tenderiser, Sweeney

surmised. I've seen them advertised on telly. Exactly the same even pattern.

Don't you ever get out of bed, Marcus sneers while ripping off his clothes, here I've been, up hill and down dale for the past two days attempting to scare up work, while you've been luxuriating like a little princess haven't you. Flaunting your wares for every Tom, Dick, and Dennis on the Land's End lot. You think you fool me, my pretty pretty, but as a matter of practical fact, you don't. I look at your face and your whole recent history's inscribed right across it like an ad for Silk Cut. That's so unfair, says Paul wanly, listlessly aroused by the sight of Marcus's lithe, muscular body as it emerges from a bewildering abundance of cloaks, sweaters, shirts, trousers, gym pants, cravats, scarves, ski hats, sweat socks, jock straps, blazers, tee-shirts, ear muffs, leather gloves, mittens, galoshes, shoes, and other less identifiable items of apparel. What's so unfair about it, Marcus wants to know, struggling with a green lurex sari belted around his waist by a black velveteen sash, you were supposed to apply for that job at the bakery, sesame sprinkler, yet I noticed the minute I got into town it's been taken, and not by you, evidently. I loved you once but you've become nothing but a drain on this existence which is hell to begin with without your type of recalcitrant mooning about dreaming of who knows what cheap scenarios. Oh Marcus, Paul sighs, applying a fingertip of Vaseline to the puckered bud Marcus fully intends to enter once he's extricated himself from the last of his profuse, expressive garments. As Marcus strips, a heavy metal object with a Bakelite grip shivers free of some confining cloth and lands with a thud on the threadbare carpet. What's that, Paul enquires sleepily. You know what it is, Marcus tells him in a deep, suggestive voice, presenting his sleek tumescence with a leer. It's your reason for living, sweetheart. I didn't mean *that*, Paul giggles, forgetting all about the object on the floor.

Dennis bites his lip as he completes his latest love letter. This time he's really sticking his neck out. 'Seth,' he's written, 'I don't know if you can possibly imagine how much you really mean to me. I think about you all the time, and with these thoughts come unassuagable desires. It would crush me if my feelings were to threaten our friendship, yet I also feel it is wrong to keep them bottled up inside, where they are killing me.' Well, Dennis thinks, maybe not killing but certainly giving me a major pain in the arse. Killing's another story. His pen poised over the airmail paper, he hears an array of creaks and groans coming from down the hall, the squealing of bedsprings, sighs and giggles, slaps, moans, cries, muffled obscenities, grunts, sobs, finally a series of loud barks, accompanied by harsh heavy breathing, everything building to a crescendo, and as he listens, as his solitude becomes unbearable, he stares helplessly at the door of his room, noticing that a stray bit of Mrs Humphreys's shawl has insinuated itself into the crack at the bottom, like some inexorable ribbon of liquorice.

You have to admit that birds are better than spiders, the diabolic Renfield asseverates, with an air of infinite reasonableness, as Pretorius makes his way to his examining chair, stepping carefully between the considerable deposits of guano decorating the cell floor. From the high barred window and the diagonal chains attached to Renfield's cot, myriad avians gaze at Pretorius, cocking their heads, cooing and gurgling in a complacent yet wary manner. A brilliantly feathered peacock struts about the cell, pecking at bread crusts. Seagulls and swallows, finches and blue jays, as well as several raptors of the owl species have been ensorcelled into Renfield's lair, God only knows how, since many of these birds are not indigenous to the area, not that Pretorius is any kind of bird expert. Clearly, though, Renfield's mania is approaching its apotheosis. Well, Renfield, Pretorius tells him, clearing his throat, quite an assortment of wildlife you've assembled, care to explain yourself?

Across the moor, in the ruined chapel of the old Bridwell place, Inspector Sweeney heaves the lid from one of the boxes of earth the shipping form says were deposited there after the wreck of the *Marlene* and sweeps the insides with the beam of his battery torch. Gnash Helviticus, the celebrated Dutch psychic who showed up in Sweeney's office only a few hours previously, insists on crumbling up some so-called consecrated wafers and dumping them into the boxes. Helviticus's accent has just about driven Sweeney up the wall, but from what he can make out, Helviticus has some Byzantine theory about the mayhem in Dullwich, claims they had an outbreak of the same sort of thing in Amsterdam, could even be the same killer, etcetera, etcetera, and he has come all this way, and Sweeney would much rather deal with this fetid-smelling wild-goose chase than contend with Madge, formerly Bobby, who's having second thoughts about going through with the final surgery, which is rather steep on his Inspector's salary, but nevertheless would put things on some normal basis, now that she's got the bazooms, keeping the rest of the old plumbing really does seem unreasonable. Is that a dog? he asks Helviticus, who's waving around a crucifix for some reason.

They are the children of the night, Helviticus snuffles, stamping the ground like a counting horse. What music they make.

Now he's eating the goddamn birds, Barney exclaims, bursting into Pretorius's sitting room with his usual lack of diplomacy. Aren't you taking your work a little bit too seriously? Pretorius teases. Relax, Barney, relax. Renfield's not even a threat to himself, let alone you. Or me.

I thought I might find you here, Inspector, Dennis says with an urgent flourish, waving his press pass in the bosky depths of the ruined Bridwell chapel. I've got a book contract, as you're probably aware.

A sea of feathers blows from the burst-open door of Renfield's vacant cell.

Don't tell *me* you haven't had your lusting eyes on that filthy writer down the hall, Marcus screeches, landing a powerful blow on the side of Paul's anaemic-looking face. I've seen the way he looks at you and the way you look at him. You *disgust* me. His vigorous slaps cause Paul's head to convulse side to side. Been down to the Whore of Dorset, haven't you? Haven't you? The glass doors to the balcony shatter into a million shards as Renfield crashes into the room, his red mouth stuffed with owl plumage that flies from his face and floats in the air as he painfully crawls through the broken glass towards Marcus.

And I suppose you've got a theory, too, like Gnash here, says Inspector Sweeney with withering insouciance. Unfortunately, criminal detection is more than a matter of fancy theories. Real lives are at stake in this case, I'm afraid, it's not like in the books you writers seem to think are the be-all, end-all. For one thing, to prove a case, you've got to have hard forensic evidence. Not just a lot of ingenious suppositions. If it was as easy as you and Helviticus seem to think, people like me would have an easy row to hoe, wouldn't we. God yes.

Pretorius snaps an amyl nitrate capsule under his nose and inhales deeply. Barney, he says, it's impossible that Renfield ate every one of those birds. It proves he's a true maniac. Now, if you were he, him, I mean, where would you make for? Whitby? The village at Land's End? Or Dullwich, where they've got all-night cafés and the like? He's got no living relatives since he murdered Myra. Virtually nobody to turn to. Unless you count this Him who is to Come he's always on about and let's face it, the man's delusional. Come to think of it, he's bound to be looking for cats. Barney partakes of the crushed capsule as if receiving the sacrament. Cats? You mean he's queer? Think he'd go to a gay bar in Dullwich? They've only got one and it's closed on Thursdays. Quite a bit more action going on right at our own Whore of Dorset after hours. No, no, no, Pretorius cackles, I mean felines. Meow, meow. After all, Barney, spiders eat flies, birds eat spiders, what eats birds?

How's this for evidence, smirks Dennis, brandishing the meat tenderiser he scooped from under Paul's bed while Marcus was using the loo. I'll bet that blood coated on it is that of the last victim, young Clotho of Burton upon Trent. Vampyre, mutters Gnash Helviticus, performing a sort of exorcising dance around the empty coffins. Yeah, yeah, Inspector Sweeney says, thinking of Madge. And where'd you happen to find this supposed instrument of mayhem? Not far away, Dennis says, I'll take you there. With Marcus put away he could have his cake and eat it too, he thought, with no fear of reprisal. And by the time Seth came around, Paul would be a thing of the past. Very much a thing of the past if his other meat tenderiser had anything to say about it.

Mrs Humphreys's got a bunch of cats, Barney exclaims, overflowing with sentience on his high. Mean little bastards if memory serves. She's been knitting a scratching post for the lot of them for the past twenty years. Keeps them in the basement, Barney says, they're wild things, they say even Doris Humphreys won't go near them without a cattle prod, they're vicious, her cats, God only knows why she keeps such vicious cats on her premises, cats are no good for protection, Dr Pretorius, as they're so fickle, they'll turn on their owner just as easily as anyone else if you provoke them. Everybody knows that as far as cats are concerned. Pretorius rubs his chin. On to the widow Humphreys's, then, he grimly commands, thinking the whole affair rather silly. Renfield will turn up like a bad penny, he always has in the past.

For twenty years, Doris Humphreys had awaited this moment. The shawl was complete as it would ever be, and at last it was time to free the little monsters in the basement. They would inherit Land's End, prowl freely its derelict streets and its stinking alleys, chew up its garbage and rid the earth of its filth. Doris had yearned and yearned and now, regardless of whatever perverted acrobatics happened to be going on upstairs, she could bid *adios* to treacle tarts and stiff breads for ever, the destiny of herself and her dear departed William lost at sea as close to closure as her mortal efforts could effect. She heard a costly lamp smashing to the floor up above, thrashing, thudding, screams, and so on, well, too bad about them, she thought, unfastening the latch on the basement door and flinging open the portal to anarchy. Puss puss, she cried into the darkness. Puss puss, come and get them.

SCOTT BRADFIELD was born in San Francisco in 1955 and now divides his time between London and the University of Connecticut, where he is Assistant Professor of English. He is the author of a novel, *The History of Luminous Motion*, *Greetings From Earth: New and Collected Stories* (Picador), and a study of American Literature, *Dreaming Revolution: Transgression in the Development of American Romance* (University of Iowa Press, 1993). He has recently completed a new novel, *What's Wrong With America*, which will be published by Picador in early 1994.

JANE DELYNN's novels include *Some Do*, *In Thrall*, *Real Estate* and *Don Juan in the Village*. The last was nominated for a Lambda award and was part of Feminist Fortnight in Britain. She's contributed to several anthologies including *High Risk: An Anthology of Forbidden Writings*. She's the librettist for the musical *Hoosick Falls* and *The Monkey Opera: The Making of a Soliloquy* (music for both by Roger Trefousse). She was in Saudi Arabia for two months writing about the Gulf War for *Mirabella* and *Rolling Stone*, and has written for *The New York Times Magazine*, *Harper's Bazaar*, *Elle*, *Decor* and *The LA Times*. She's an avid scuba diver and swimmer and currently teaches writing at Lehman College, CUNY, in New York.

ALISON FELL is a Scottish poet and novelist who lives in London. Her poetry collections are *Kisses for Mayakovsky* and *The Crystal Owl*, and her novels include *Every Move You Make* and *Mer de Glace*, which won the 1991 Boardman Tasker Award for Mountain Literature. She has edited and contributed to three women's collections, *The Seven Deadly Sins*, *The Seven Cardinal Virtues* and *Serious Hysterics*.

PENELOPE FITZGERALD was brought up in Sussex and Hampstead and educated at Somerville College, Oxford. She is a biographer and novelist, and was awarded the Booker Prize in 1979 for *Offshore*, and the Rose Mary Crawshay Prize in 1985 for *Charlotte Mew and Her Friends*, a life of the poet. *Offshore* was based on her experiences of living in a houseboat on the Thames in the 1960s; unfortunately it sank. She has three children and nine grandchildren, and does a certain amount of travelling. In 1991 she went to Tasmania for their Writers' Festival, and was given the idea for the story 'The Means of Escape'.

NINA FITZPATRICK's collection of short stories *Fables of the Irish Intelligentsia* was awarded the Irish Times–Aer Lingus award for best first book by an Irish author in 1991. The prize was subsequently withdrawn on the grounds that the author could not prove Irish citizenship. FitzPatrick describes herself as a wondering 'scholar gypsy' dividing her time between Ireland, Poland and Norway. She's currently working on an adventure novel set in Eastern European 'Absurdistan'.

GARY INDIANA is the author of three novels, *Horse Crazy*, *Gone Tomorrow* and *Rent Boy*, and two collections of stories, *Scar Tissue* and *White Trash Boulevard*. He lives in New York City.

PENELOPE LIVELY is a novelist and short story writer. Her novel *Moon Tiger* won the Booker Prize in 1987. Her other books include *Pack of Cards*, a collection of short stories. Penelope Lively was born in Egypt and spent her childhood there before coming to England in 1945. She now lives in London and Oxfordshire.

MARSHA ROWE first came to Britain in 1969 from Sydney. She worked on *OZ* magazine and *INK* before co-founding the feminist magazine, *Spare Rib*. She edited the *Spare Rib Reader*, the anthology of the first ten years. Her previous anthologies of short stories are *Sex and the City*, *So Very English* and *Sacred Space*. She has contributed essays and stories to various anthologies, and is currently researching and writing *Breath*, a book about asthma. She lives in London and is married with one daughter.

COLM TÓIBÍN was born in Ireland in 1955. He lives in Dublin. His novels are *The South* (1990) and *The Heather Blazing* (1992). His other books are *Walking Along the Border* (1987), *Homage to Barcelona* (1990) and a collection of journalism, *The Trial of the Generals* (1990).

DAVID WIDGERY was born in London in 1947 and qualified in medicine in 1974. He died in 1992. He was the author of six books including *Beating Time*, *Preserving Disorder* and *Some Lives* and was co-editor of *The Chatto Book of Dissent*. He lived with the fashion historian Juliet Ash and two children in Hackney.